RESCUED
BY HER BEAR
BLACK RIDGE BEARS BOOK 2

FELICITY HEATON

THE BLACK RIDGE BEARS SERIES

Book 1: Stolen by her Bear

Book 2: Rescued by her Bear

Book 3: Saved by her Bear

Book 4: Unleashed by her Bear

Book 5: Awakened by her Bear

The Black Ridge Bears series is part of the Eternal Mates World, which includes the Eternal Mates series, Cougar Creek Mates series, and the London Vampires series.

Discover more available paranormal romance books at:
http://www.felicityheaton.com

Or sign up to my mailing list to receive a FREE vampire romance ebook, learn about new titles, be eligible for special subscriber-only giveaways, and read exclusive content including short stories:
http://ml.felicityheaton.com/mailinglist

CHAPTER 1

Cameo couldn't believe the turn her life had taken. Being on the run from a drug cartel had not been in her binder, but apparently she couldn't plan everything that was going to happen to her. She swallowed her desire to curse as she kept her eyes fixed on her boots, carefully watching her footing as she navigated a particularly treacherous stretch of the narrow dirt trail that cut through the forest, hugging the base of a steep white mountain.

Even though she tried to keep her focus on not falling into the pines and firs that lined the slope to her right, part of it kept drifting to behind her. She tensed and froze as a sound echoed through the forest and she imagined someone was there, closing in on her. Her heart lodged in her throat, hammering there, and her breaths came faster, fogging in the chilly air. She resisted the urge to hurry onwards and started slowly moving again. Rushing was a sure-fire way of making herself trip and if she fell and hurt herself out here, only one of three things was going to happen.

She would freeze to death.

One of the local predators would eat her.

Or the men she was sure were following her would catch her.

Cameo breathed hard as the trail narrowed even further and sharply began to ascend to a part of the forest where the trees were sparser and the snow had been able to settle on the ground. She held back another curse. This wasn't good.

Her breath misted in the air in front of her face as she picked her way over a tangled root that crossed the path, gripped a whip-thin sapling with her left hand and eased along a section of trail that had a sharp downwards angle to it that made her feel the mountain was determined to hurl her off it. Sweat dampened her brow beneath her thick woollen hat, irritating her. She wanted to wipe it away, but she wasn't about to remove her gloves. The temperature was declining rapidly as the afternoon wore on and she couldn't afford to lose any more of her body heat. She wasn't sure she would be able to light a fire to warm up when it got too dark for her to continue.

They might see it.

They might find her.

Cameo wasn't sure how they had caught up with her.

Back in Banff, she had been sure she had lost them, had started to relax while stocking up on supplies and had even spent the night in a motel, but then a red SUV had tailed her rental to the outskirts of the town and hadn't left her rear view for close to fifty miles. When she had taken a precautionary detour to prove to herself that she was just being jittery and she wasn't being followed, the SUV had remained on her tail.

Cameo had panicked and tried to lose them, had made it far enough ahead of them that they would have lost sight of her on the winding highway, and had turned down another road.

She had picked a doozy.

The road she had thought would lead her north towards another main road had led her to what amounted to little more than a forestry track. Recent tyre tracks had given her hope that she would find a cabin somewhere at the end of it, some place where she could call for help even when she hated the thought of pulling anyone into danger. When she had reached the end of the track, there had been several vehicles parked there, all of them covered in snow.

Cameo had parked her car next to them, dressed quickly for the weather and grabbed her backpack, and hadn't stuck around. She had headed into the mountains, following a trail at first, but she lost it somewhere in the woods as a storm had closed in and had ended up taking a quick break to check the map in her pack.

She had checked her position on her GPS five times and had eventually ended up cursing.

It turned out that the valley she had picked only had one building marked on it and it was across the other side of the valley, miles from where she was.

She breathed a sigh of relief when she found a trail that led downwards before she reached the snowline, followed that instead and remained on guard, listening for signs of life in the forest. There had to be someone living out here. Those cars had been there for some time and the footprints in the snow had led in this direction, not towards the other side of the valley.

She glanced up the mountain. Maybe if she could climb a little higher, where she could see above the tops of the trees, she might be able to spot a cabin nearby.

Probably not. Snow whizzed across the mountain, obscuring the peak of it, and the storm was only getting worse. Soon, it would be a blizzard. Climbing higher to see anything in this weather was not only dangerous, but pointless. She wouldn't be able to see a few feet in front of her face.

Cameo rubbed her right arm, trying to keep the chill off it as the wind buffeted her and snow bit into her face as the gale drove it through the trees. Her thick dark green coat and black pants had been made for this weather, but she still felt the bitter bite of the cold. Her toes were numb in her waterproof boots, despite the thermal fleece that lined them, and her fingers felt ready to fall off.

She looked up as the light began to fade and told herself that she didn't need to be worried when a jolt of fear jangled her veins and chilled her blood. Bears would be asleep at this time of year. Although that left her with wolves and cougars to worry about.

She chuckled mirthlessly.

And humans.

She looked back over her shoulder, peering into the gloomy forest, trying to see past the snow that made it through the canopy, falling in great chunks in places as wind shook the pines. She sent up a silent prayer that she had been mistaken even when she knew she wasn't. It was them. The same men who had threatened her. Maybe they would keep going on the highway or not think to check the road she had taken. Maybe they were right on her tail, hidden just beyond that ridge she could see.

How was she going to get out of this one? If she kept going, she was only moving deeper into dangerous territory. She didn't have enough food to keep her alive for long, although the cold would probably kill her before hunger did. If she didn't keep going, there was a chance the men would catch her, and that didn't bear thinking about.

She could call the authorities.

But part of her was still convinced that was a wrong move and would end with her being in more trouble than she was right now. The cartel, or whatever they called themselves, had made it clear that her parents would end up just like her brother if she spoke with anyone.

She couldn't keep going like this though. Even if she evaded them, eventually they would catch her, or worse, they would go after her parents to make her give herself up.

She fished her phone from her pocket and checked it, her hands shaking as the screen lit up. No signal. Calling for help wasn't an option after all. She tried to stop herself, but her thumb moved to the messages and pressed on the icon, and sickness rolled through her as she opened one of them.

Cameo stared at the picture they had sent her, one that had made her vomit when she had first seen it, still terrified and tormented her now.

Nate, her younger brother, was unrecognisable in it, slumped in a chair with his arms bound behind his back, covered in blood.

Dead.

She couldn't let that happen to her parents.

Wouldn't let that happen to her.

Cameo closed the message and shoved the phone back in the pocket of her salopettes, shifting the canister of bear spray that hung from her belt aside. She paused and leaned against one of the towering pines, breathing hard as she struggled not to vomit. When they had sent that photograph to her, she had been convinced it was some sort of terrible joke, the kind her brother would play on her.

When two men had shown up at her door and threatened her, she had realised it was real.

Nate was dead and now the cartel he had worked for was after her, all because he had told them she had the money they wanted.

She didn't.

Her brother had always been a wild card, had always done crazy things, the complete opposite of her as he had rolled with the punches and seen where the wind would blow him, but she had honestly thought he had put that life behind him.

When he had moved from the small sleepy hamlet where they had grown up on the east coast to busy Vancouver eight years ago, she had loved having him nearby, had visited him often at first.

But then her job as a park ranger had taken her out of the city and into the heart of the Rocky Mountains.

Cameo had thought he had been doing well.

And then he had come to visit her with some of his 'friends' and had tried to convince her to use her connections as a ranger to help them move drugs across the border, whether it was by land or sea.

She should have seen then how desperate he was, trying to prove his worth to the neatly dressed thugs he had brought with him.

As a ranger, she came across her fair share of illegally planted pot in the forests up in the mountains, but what her brother had been involved in was something else, and he had been in deep. Before she could find a way to get him out, he had gotten himself killed, and the people he had worked for had come after her.

Demanding she pay them the three hundred grand her brother owed them.

Cameo turned and sagged against the tree, her breath leaving her on a sigh that turned to mist in front of her face.

And she had discovered who had gotten Nate involved in such a shady business in the first place.

Karl.

Her ex.

The ex.

The only man she had ever really fallen in love with. It had broken her heart when she had put an end to things between them when her application to become a ranger, something she had always wanted to be, had been accepted. Karl had refused to come with her across the country.

He had expected her to give up her dream.

Had been angry when she had refused.

Things between them had ended on a bad note and now it was all the worse. Now she was running for her life, fearing her parents might be doing the same. The message Karl had sent had made it clear that if she didn't get them the money, what had happened to Nate would happen to her parents.

Cameo had immediately messaged her father and told them to head to the remote cabin they owned close to Moose Lake, one that had been in the family for generations. She didn't think Karl knew about it. She had certainly never told him.

And then she had gone on the run.

She frowned as darkness closed in around her, as the temperature dropped sharply, and tilted her head back as she stepped away from the tree, peering up through the dense canopy to the sky. The clouds were lower now, thick and heavy. It looked like more snow was coming. Just great. Just her luck. At this rate, even the forest floor would be covered in a deep layer of it.

She debated whether to keep moving or to stop for the night. She had a flashlight so she could find her way, but darkness wasn't the thing she was worried about. It was the local wildlife. A flashlight wasn't going to scare off wolves or a hungry cougar if they were prowling around in this storm, desperate to eat. Fire was her better option.

Plus, she was cold to the bone now, and hungry. If she didn't rest, she would probably collapse somewhere out there in the dark.

Resting and eating were worth the risk of being spotted. It was important she keep her strength up. Maybe, if she was lucky, the men wouldn't come and in the morning she could circle her way back to her car and check it out from a distance to make sure it wasn't being watched.

She scoured the forest, trying to find a good spot to set up camp. Maybe her luck was changing for the better. There was a hollow beneath the sprawling roots of a fallen tree. It would provide shelter from the blizzard and make it harder for predators to sneak up on her.

Cameo shrugged out of her heavy pack and set it down inside the small earth cave. Her stiff fingers made opening it hard work, but she managed it and pulled out everything she needed for a small fire. She had come prepared, had packed everything she might need to survive in the wild before she had left home. Protein bars. Her water purifying bottle. Thermal layers. Spare gloves and another scarf. Crampons for her boots. Even her sleeping bag and bedroll.

At least life as a ranger had prepared her for surviving while on the run in the mountains.

She gathered what dry wood she could find and made a fire just at the mouth of the earth cave, lit it and watched smoke rise lazily in the air and catch on the wind that carried it south. The fire flickered and guttered, almost going out as a stronger breeze swept around her, but it sprang back to life as the direction of the wind changed again, coming from directly behind the cave.

Cameo grabbed a protein bar from her pack and closed it again, turned the bag and used it as a seat. She stared at the fire as she ate and sipped her water, savoured the warmth of the flames as they flickered and danced. Hopefully, it would be enough to deter the predators. If it wasn't, then she would use her bear spray.

She fished her phone out of her pocket again and looked at the messages from her father. The last few dozen messages were the same—a heart he sent every morning to let her know that they were fine. She had missed sending one back to him this morning and hoped he wasn't worried about her.

She set up a heart in a message and added 'bad signal' and pressed the send button. It would go when she had signal and hopefully it would ease her parents' minds.

She pocketed her phone and huddled down into her coat, and tried to stay awake, but fatigue rolled up on her and her adrenaline crashed as silence stretched around her. She blinked as her eyelids slipped closed, widened her eyes and sucked down a breath, and then another, hoping the chilly air in her lungs would wake her up.

It didn't.

Sleep overcame her.

When she woke, it was almost dark. She huffed and chastised herself, pushed to her feet and grimaced as her leg muscles cramped and ached. She stomped her feet to get some warmth back into them, hoping to wake herself up.

Something behind her cracked.

Her hand flew to her bear spray as she whirled to face the direction of the sound, her pulse skyrocketing as images of cougars or wolves filled her mind.

It was worse.

It turned out her luck wasn't getting better after all.

She stared at the two men dressed in heavy black weatherproof gear, panic lancing her and flooding her veins with adrenaline that made her shake.

The very thugs she had thought had been tailing her.

The one on the left checked his rifle over, his hazel eyes as cold as the snow that whipped through the trees around them.

The one to the right smiled as he aimed a pistol at her.

"Hello, Cameo."

CHAPTER 2

Lowe kept pace with his twin brother, Knox, following the snowy trail through the woods, his thoughts keeping him silent as they headed north towards the lodge near the glacier at the head of the valley. Something was wrong with their alpha, Saint. The big bear shifter was caught up in a female he had kidnapped from the neighbouring cougars, had turned on Knox and then demanded he and Lowe get the lodge ready so he could move her there.

If it had been summer, Lowe wouldn't have minded as much. Hell, if the weather had been clear, he wouldn't have minded as much.

But it was blowing a gale and the snow was falling thick and fast, and even the forest didn't offer much protection from the storm. The snow had managed to work its way into the heart of the pines and formed a layer a few inches thick on the ground that made it hard going. He wasn't a cougar or a wolf, wasn't nimble on his feet like that breed of shifter. Maintaining his footing was requiring constant focus, and it was making him grouchy.

Knox muttered things beneath his breath beside him, grumbling about Saint and the female.

Lowe glanced across at his brother, reached out when the need to calm him became too great and laid a gloved hand on his wide shoulders.

Knox's stormy blue eyes slid to him and then he huffed, faced forwards again and growled. "Can't see shit in this weather."

Lowe knew the snow wasn't the reason Knox was in a foul mood. He wasn't happy about being sent away by Saint either, but he would do as his alpha ordered. He preferred to go with the flow rather than cause any aggravation, unlike Knox. Knox had wanted to fight Saint when he had ordered them to prepare the lodge, but Lowe had calmed him down.

"Don't know how you can be so relaxed about this. It isn't right. Saint's head isn't on straight where this female is concerned," Knox rumbled and kicked at a fallen branch, sending it flying out of his way.

Lowe smiled tightly. He might be calm on the surface, but his bear side was as grumpy as Knox. His more human side and his bear one had always been polar opposites. He wasn't sure that part of him knew how to be calm. It was always easily agitated, always alert, and right now it was uneasy.

Something didn't feel right, and he wasn't talking about Saint and the cougar female now.

He glanced around the woods, peering through the endless sea of trunks.

Something didn't feel right in the valley.

He couldn't put a name to it, but it had him on edge and had his bear side restless, constantly scanning the area trying to figure out what was wrong. He glanced at Knox again, torn between mentioning it and keeping it to himself. His younger brother would only shrug it off and put it down to Saint and their frigid trek to the lodge.

And the fact they were all awake in the dead of winter.

An image of his bed popped into his head, heavy with warm furs and stacked with soft pillows.

He growled, aching to crawl under the layers of sheets and sleep.

Beside him, Knox chuckled. "Thinking about somewhere warm and dry, too?"

Lowe nodded. "Maybe once we're done getting the place set up, we can bed down at the lodge."

"Fuck, that sounds good." Knox rolled his shoulders and huffed again, his breath fogging in the air as he glared at the snow that made it through the trees and swirled towards them. His dark blond eyebrows knitted hard. "Get out of this shit. Get the lodge ready. Get a few drinks in us, maybe thaw a steak or two and hit the sack... away from the noisy cougars."

That sounded more than good. It sounded heavenly.

Their noisy neighbours were the reason they were in this mess, had woken him, Knox and Saint from their winter sleep with some kind of pride celebration. Knox suspected it was a wedding. Well, if their alpha had anything to do with it, it was going ahead without one of the cougars.

Saint hadn't exactly handled the rude awakening with decorum.

The whole affair had agitated Lowe's bear side even further and had irritated Knox to the point where he wasn't thinking straight. Lowe glanced at his brother, feeling the weight of responsibility settling on his shoulders. He needed to calm Knox, to ease him down, and he knew just the way to do it.

Lowe focused on mentally preparing those steaks in his head, trying to remember what they had in storage up at the lodge. There were three things his brother needed in order to relax, and all three awaited them at the quiet lodge.

Steaks. Whiskey. Sleep.

His bear side groaned at the latter.

All he wanted was to go back to bed, to sleep the winter away as he did every year. All he wanted was for things to remain peaceful at Black Ridge. But here he was, trekking through the snow, battling the adverse weather conditions, because his damned alpha had gotten it into his head that stealing a female from the cougars as revenge for waking his pride from their winter sleep was a grand plan.

Gods, Lowe should have told him to take her back the second Saint had marched into the Ridge with her.

He had wanted to, but Saint was his alpha, and he was a good one. The big male had taken care of him and Knox, had provided a home for them when they had badly needed one, and had brought them into the pride.

A pride that might be makeshift, mostly filled with bears gathered from various clans, but it was a pride nonetheless.

A family.

One that felt as if it was stronger and meant more to those in it because it was made up of bears who had come together to live as a group. The bond between him and Saint, and Maverick and Rune, felt stronger than the bonds he'd had with bears who had been part of his old pride, ones tied together by blood and tradition. Those bonds had been flimsy, had snapped with only the slightest pressure, leaving him and Knox without a home.

A home they had found with Saint and the others. A family that shared a powerful bond that felt unbreakable. He would do anything for the males in his pride and he knew they would do anything for him.

And that was why he was freezing his ass off trekking to a remote lodge.

Saint needed him to do this, and so he would do it.

"Think maybe we have any butter in the freezer?" Lowe's mouth watered as he thought about a nice perfectly cooked rib-eye brushed with butter and cracked black peppercorns.

Knox chuckled again, the warm sound soothing Lowe. His brother's mood was improving even if the weather wasn't. He gritted his teeth and braced as a blast of icy wind battered him, dug his heavy boots in to keep himself upright. When it passed, he brushed the snow off his black jacket and trudged onwards.

"Typical of you to think about the food first." Knox jabbed him on his arm. "I was thinking about the whiskey."

"Aren't you always?" Lowe slid him a look, grinned at him. "Bourbon glaze might be nice."

"Oh gods, honey and bourbon glazed steak." Knox smacked his lips together, his blue eyes losing their focus as a dreamy look crossed his face.

Knox had never been able to resist either honey or what he called the 'dark nectar of the gods'. Once, one particularly fine and long summer back when they had been younger, he had witnessed Knox in his bear form running from a swarm of bees with half a hive stuck on his head and chunks of honey flying from him in all directions.

He had never let his brother live that one down.

He had honestly never seen anything funnier than a five-hundred-plus pound grizzly thundering along a wooded riverbank trying to outrun angry bees.

"You know I can practically feel you thinking about it. Quit it," Knox growled in his direction.

Lowe fought the smile that wanted to curve his lips as his brother glared at him, pulled a face and tugged his black scarf up to his nose when he couldn't hold back the smile any longer.

"Two honey and bourbon glazed steaks coming right up." Lowe patted his brother on his back again, hoping he wouldn't hold on to his bad mood.

"Make it four." Knox rubbed his stomach through his own black winter jacket. "I'll be fiendishly hungry by the time we get there."

Knox was always fiendishly hungry. It was a good job Lowe loved cooking as much as he did. His brother had one hell of an appetite.

It dawned on him that his uneasy feeling had passed thanks to losing himself in conversation and tried to think of another topic to keep his mind occupied. Other than Knox and the bees. Food stuck in his head, tormenting him, keeping his pace brisk despite the slippery ground.

"I probably should've thawed a few steaks for Saint." He glanced at Knox, whose look said it all.

Saint hadn't exactly been in the mood to have them sticking around though, had wanted them gone because Knox had scared the female.

"What happened back there?" Lowe rubbed his hands together, trying to get some warmth into them. His gloves were good, but apparently not that good. The tips of his fingers were already cold.

Knox shrugged and growled. "Saint chewed me a new one. He probably should've asked you to watch the female."

"Yeah, well, I probably would've let her escape." Lowe felt his brother's gaze on the side of his face, pushed his woollen hat back and ran a hand over his short blond hair as he sighed. "Just... it doesn't sit well with me."

"Always the gentleman." Knox took another jab at his arm and grinned at him, flashing straight white teeth. "Mom always said you were the nice one out of the two of us, and I was too much like Dad."

They both fell silent at that.

When that silence became too thick, started to feel as if it was choking him, Lowe forced a sigh and tilted his head back, gazing up through the canopy to the grey sky.

"I miss them."

Knox wrapped his arm around Lowe's shoulders and tugged him towards him. "Me too."

Lowe lifted his left hand and patted his brother's gloved hand. It had been hard for both of them when they had lost their parents. Things had changed at their old pride on the coast just north of Vancouver and they had ended up striking out on their own, trying to find a place that felt like home to them.

They thought they had found it in a small cabin they had built near a lake, had settled there and things had been good for a while.

Until they had been out in their bear forms and Knox had been shot by hunters. They had shifted back and had run as far as Knox could manage. When his brother hadn't been able to keep going, had collapsed and terrified Lowe, Lowe had started dragging him, trying to get him to help. Lowe's throat closed as he remembered finding himself at a point where two valleys converged, sitting with his brother and too tired to keep moving.

He could still recall how it had felt to sit there looking at Knox, sure he was going to die.

And then Saint had appeared.

Lowe had attacked him, hadn't been able to stop himself from shifting into his animal form to protect his brother, even though he had sensed Saint was a bear too.

When Saint had offered to help save Knox, Lowe had been more than grateful. Saint had helped him move Knox to Black Ridge, had set them up in a cabin and had let them stay there until his brother had healed and was back at full strength.

And then, just when Lowe and Knox had decided it was time they moved on, even when neither of them had wanted to, the big bear had offered them both a place in his pride.

They owed Saint everything, but somehow the male didn't make them feel like they did. He had never treated them as if they owed him anything, rarely pulled rank on them, and always took care of them. From day one, Saint had made them feel as if they belonged in his pride, as if Black Ridge had always been their home, and as if they had always known each other.

"You're awfully quiet." Knox nudged him as they reached an area where the trees were sparse and the snow was deeper.

Lowe couldn't stop himself from glancing at Knox's right shoulder.

His brother's blue eyes widened slightly. "Ah... winter silence making you all contemplative? Or is this because Saint gave me a spanking for upsetting the female?"

Lowe shrugged. "I'm going to blame the cold. Must be freezing my brain and making me sentimental."

Knox scoffed at that. "You don't need the cold for that to happen. For a big bear, you're a big softie. You know that?"

He wanted to deny that, but their mother had been right about him. Lowe was the gentler one out of the two of them and sometimes he wished it wasn't the case—like the times he got his heart broken.

Knox had never had his heart broken. Knox could somehow roll into town or Vancouver, find a female to fool around with to blow off some steam, and escape with his heart intact.

Whenever Lowe tried that, it started out well, and then ended badly. He tried not to let his feelings get involved, tried to keep things fast and fun like Knox could, and then more often than not he ended up foolishly developing feelings and thinking he could make a relationship work.

It never did.

"I know that look," Knox grumbled. "It's that female. I don't like her. She's messing everything up. First Saint is acting all crazy, and now you look miserable."

Lowe shrugged again, trying to let it roll off his back. "I told you I was done with trying to make things work with females. No more. Last two years, I haven't had any problems."

"Last two years you've had precisely one encounter with a female. I don't call that progress."

He slid Knox a hard look. "I don't see you out there sowing your wild oats. When was the last time you went to town to get laid? Two years ago now?"

"I've been busy." Knox glowered at him, but before he looked away, Lowe glimpsed something in his blue eyes, something that looked an awful lot like hurt.

Was it possible he and his brother weren't so different after all, and Knox's last visit to town to find a female had ended badly for him?

He wanted to know, but he also didn't want to press his brother. Knox could hold a grudge like no other man in this world, wouldn't talk to him for months if he went prodding the bear and aggravated him.

"Weather's getting worse." Knox didn't sound happy about it either. "How close do you think we are to the lodge now?"

Lowe zipped his coat up a little more as the icy wind battered him, driving snow into his face, and looked back over his shoulder, into a blizzard that stole everything from view. "Not sure. Might be halfway there. It's hard to tell. It's got to be late afternoon now. Maybe close to evening. I feel like I've been walking forever."

"Me too. Not sure we'll make it to the lodge before nightfall, but I'm fucked if I'm stopping anywhere for the night. We'll just have to keep our spirits up while we walk." Knox growled as the wind caught him, splattering his weatherproof clothing with snow, and stomped onwards. "Tell me more about steaks and whiskey."

Lowe chuckled as his brother sounded as if this was the end for them. He hated snow as much as any bear, but it wasn't that bad. Things could be worse.

A gunshot echoed around the mountains.

His entire body locked up tight. Knox froze too, head whipping in all directions. Lowe tried to get a fix on the location of whoever had fired that shot, but it was impossible. He strained and waited, senses reaching outwards, sweeping as far and wide as possible to cover as much ground as he could manage. He couldn't sense anyone other than him and Knox, and a few animals in the dense forest. He remained on high alert though. Whoever had fired that shot was bound to shoot again, giving Lowe a chance to get a fix on them.

"You think it's the cougars?" It sounded stupid now he had said it. Shifters didn't use guns. It just wasn't the done thing. But he was worried about Saint.

"Nah." Knox slowly turned to face the way they had come, looking back towards the Ridge. "Cougars are crazy, but they're not that crazy. Quit worrying about Saint. As long as this storm is raging, he's safe."

His brother was probably right. The cougars were unlikely to go out searching for the female while the weather was like this. They would wait for it to pass and then they would track her down, and then Saint would be in trouble. Only crazy people would be out in this weather.

"Who do you think it was then?" Lowe scanned the mountain to his left, his gut saying the sound had come from that direction.

Knox bluntly said, "Hunters."

Another shot rang out and confirmed Lowe's feeling that it had come from their left. He tried to narrow it down more, but all he could do was guess. Either way, it was too close for comfort. He closed ranks with his brother, coming to stand slightly in front of him to shield him. Knox huffed at that.

"Humans are crazy, do stupid stuff like thinking they can handle a storm like this without it killing them, but in all the years we've lived here, no human has ever dared to come up this way to hunt in the dead of winter. There's nothing awake here at this time of year." Lowe glanced over his shoulder at Knox. "You don't think it's... Archangel?"

He had never personally encountered the hunter organisation that specialised in dealing with what they called 'non-humans' but he had heard the horror stories from numerous immortals in his years, and he had heard first-hand accounts of them from Saint, Rune and Maverick.

Archangel had held Rune and Maverick for decades in an underground arena where they had been forced to fight other immortals in cage matches. Slaves to the humans, made to kill each other for entertainment. Lowe didn't even want to imagine what their lives had been like. Thankfully, Saint had participated in a raid on one compound in Vancouver and had freed them, and they had joined the pride.

Lowe wouldn't exactly say Rune and Maverick were recovering from their ordeal. Sometimes, both bears had a cold, dead look in their eyes that warned everyone away from them. Sometimes, Rune and Maverick ended up brawling over the slightest thing, and Saint had to step in to stop them once it started to go too far.

The rest of the time, the two bears were thick as thieves, as close as brothers could be without the blood to link them. Hell, maybe even closer than siblings could be. They shared a strong bond, one forged in that crucible, in whatever hell they had gone through and emerged from together.

Their bond was as powerful as the one Lowe shared with his twin.

A bond that was relaying how on edge Knox was right now.

Knox came to stand beside him and glared in the direction of the mountain. "I doubt it. Archangel haven't dared come up this way since the cougars ran them off. It's probably just a bunch of kids from town with too much testosterone, borrowing daddy's hunting rifle and trying to impress some females."

It wouldn't be the first time that had happened. Saint had scared away a fair number of groups of youths in his time. Normally they came up in summer though.

"What are they meant to be hunting in all this snow?" Lowe looked across at his brother.

Knox shrugged.

"Don't know. Don't care." He pointed to tracks in the snow a short distance from them. "Moose maybe?"

Lowe was worried they were after more than the local ungulates. "What if they're after the bears?"

One year, soon after he and Knox had settled at the Ridge, a group of adult males had come up to shoot bears in early spring while they had been asleep in their dens. He shifted from foot to foot as he remembered that day, his bear side restless with a need to hunt down whoever was on the mountain and deal with them as he had those hunters. They hadn't made it back to town.

Saint had buried their bodies deep in the forest on the other side of the valley with Rune and Maverick's help, and none of them had spoken about it since.

Knox had been given the unenviable task of talking Lowe down, convincing him to shift back from his bear form, and had a few scars to show for it. Lowe hadn't been able to stop himself from lashing out at anyone who had come near the dead female black bear and her tiny squirming cubs that had been crawling on her, calling for her.

In the end, it had been Rune who had managed to convince Lowe to shift back. A big cinnamon black bear himself, he had been as angry as Lowe to see what the hunters had done to an innocent mother.

Rune had shown a softer side that still seemed impossible, had bundled up the two cubs in his jacket and had taken them back to the Ridge, and had ended up raising them both in his cabin. The two females had grown up strong and healthy, and after a few years of being tutored by their adoptive cinnamon bear father, they had gone on their way.

Sometimes, they dropped by the Ridge in summer.

Lowe had been moved to tears the first time one had shown up with cubs in tow. Rune had demanded she tell him who the hell had knocked her up and had then proceeded to roll around on the stone bank of the creek with them, playing until both cubs had been exhausted.

Everyone at the Ridge knew where the sisters overwintered and Saint always went to check on the two of them when they woke. Lowe worried that one spring soon, Saint was going to come back with bad news. Wild bears didn't have anywhere near the same lifespan as their shifter counterparts.

He looked to his brother, needing to hear him say that the hunters weren't after the bears, and wind whipped against him.

Laced with the faintest hint of blood.

"You smell that?" Lowe frowned in the direction of the mountain.

Knox stared hard at it too, blue eyes scanning the blizzard and the shadowy shapes of the trees.

He muttered, "I smell it. Guess we have our answer now. The humans are hunting each other."

Lowe pulled down a deeper breath as wind gusted against him. He caught the scent more clearly and every muscle in his body clamped down onto his bones as an urge to growl rolled through him, hitting him out of nowhere.

A third shot rang out.

Lowe kicked off, sprinting through the trees in the direction it had come from.

"Come back!" Knox yelled.

Lowe couldn't.

He needed to find the source of that scent, before he was too late.

Before whoever was after her ended up killing her.

CHAPTER 3

Cameo was quick to release the bear spray and depress the trigger. Her aim was a little off, caught only the man with the rifle. He roared in agony and stumbled backwards, fumbling with his gun as he raised his hands to his face, and she flinched and tensed as the loud crack of it firing made her ears ring. She broke into a sprint as the second man moved, running to her left, placing the injured man between her and the one with the pistol.

He hollered something at her that she didn't hear over her fast breaths, over her heart as it thundered in her aching ears. She just kept running, winding through the trees, trying to use them for cover as her mind raced. What was she going to do?

Adrenaline surged, had her blood pumping faster as she squinted into the snow that rushed towards her and battled the fierce wind. Her legs ached but she kept running, trying to see the path ahead of her, pushing herself past her limit as fear gripped her. She had to keep running. It didn't matter where she ended up. She would deal with that once she had escaped.

Her panted breaths didn't get a chance to fog the air as she raced forwards into an area where the trees thinned.

The weather was worse than she had thought possible, the wind and snow so intense and the darkness falling so rapidly that she could barely make out what was a few feet from her. It slowed her, but hopefully it would cover her tracks too, would make it hard for the man she hadn't hit with the bear spray to find her. He would be coming after her while his companion tried to shake off the effects of the spray.

Maybe she could disappear in this storm and find a place to shelter, one where he wouldn't find her.

She risked looking back.

Gasped as she saw a light bobbing around behind her, chasing after her through the snow.

She had to go faster.

Cameo pushed herself harder, running blindly as panic took the helm, and regretted it when she ended up following another wrong route, heading higher into the trees with no way of getting down without a long slide down a steep, wooded slope. She would probably break something if she went down there, and she couldn't turn back either. All she could do was keep going and hope there was a route down again and this trail didn't just lead up to the mountain.

The snow grew deeper, covering the trail, forcing her to slow down and watch her step. She panted hard as she carefully walked, kicking snow aside so she could see the path. Her trembling legs made it hard work and the glances she kept tossing at the thirty-foot drop to her right weren't helping. She couldn't seem to convince her eyes to remain on the path though. That drop kept beckoning her.

Pain blazed across her left arm before she even heard the gunshot.

Cameo flinched and stumbled, landed on her hands and knees on the trail. She forced herself to stand again, covered the rip in her coat with her right hand and pushed herself to keep going. It had been a wild shot—a lucky shot. That was all. If she just kept going, she would be fine.

She couldn't stop herself from slowing though as her blood seemed to chill and her mind started to blank and her legs felt like noodles beneath her.

A shriek tore from her lips as the man grabbed her right arm and twisted her towards him. She hit him with her left arm and gritted her teeth as the fire burning across her biceps blazed hotter.

She clenched her jaw and kept hitting him, desperately trying to break free, images of her brother flashing across her mind as fear swamped her. She was going to end up like that—beaten and dead.

No. She couldn't let it happen. She fumbled, trying to reach her bear spray.

The man shoved her to the ground, into the snow, and jammed the gun in her face.

Freezing her.

"Tell me where the money is, bitch." He squeezed her left arm.

Cameo whimpered and screwed her eyes shut, but refused to cry out as pain rolled through her, making her nauseous.

"Tell me where it is." He growled those words.

She looked up at him. "I don't have any money. Nate was lying to you. He probably thought you would let him go… was desperate. I don't have any money."

Cameo could see in his dark eyes that he didn't believe her, that he was never going to believe her. She stifled another cry as he dragged her onto her feet, using his grip on her left arm to lever her up off the snow.

He glared down at her. "Karl will deal with you. He'll be arriving in a couple of days."

Panic blasted through her. Karl had been the one who had beaten her brother to death. Sweet Karl who had turned into a bastard when he had become an adult. She had been shocked when she had discovered he had gotten into the drug business, hadn't wanted to believe the things Nate had told her, but now she did.

Karl was as sadistic as her brother had painted him.

And he was going to kill her when he realised she didn't have his money.

And then he would kill her parents.

"March." The man shoved her past him on the track, back the way they had come.

Cameo jerked backwards and hit the man with an elbow to the face, only meant to knock him away from her so she could run.

He stumbled, bellowed as he fell backwards and tugged her towards the edge of the path. She grabbed one of the trees and clung to it, holding on for dear life as his weight pulled her with him, and then relief rushed through her as he lost his grip.

Relief that swiftly became guilt as she looked down the slope, watched him strike a tree and get spun around.

His flashlight twirled, blinding her before it clattered down to the bottom of the slope ahead of him. His gun went off as he hit another and she flinched and curled into a ball, grimaced as he tumbled and landed against a tree at the bottom of the slope, his body bent backwards at an awful angle.

Cameo released the tree and twisted to face the slope, the cold uneven ground biting into her hands and knees. She eased forwards, peering down at him as she breathed hard, trying to see him more clearly through the darkness.

Dread pooled in her stomach.

In the weak glow of the flashlight that had landed facing him, he wasn't moving and blood tracked down his forehead from a nasty wound on his temple.

He couldn't be dead.

Oh God, she couldn't have killed a man.

She leaned further forwards, desperately seeking a sign of life.

Shrieked as her left hand slipped, fumbled for the tree nearest her and missed it.

She hit the slope on her chest, somehow managed to spin herself around and roll onto her back so she was sliding feet first instead. Her lungs felt too tight as she desperately tried to control her descent, reaching for trees and roots, anything to stop herself.

Her left leg hit a tree, the impact jarring, and she cried out as fire rolled up her bones. She ended up spinning around again, into an uncontrolled roll that had her tumbling down the rest of the slope.

Cameo slid to a halt beneath a pine and laid there on her back, breathing hard, snow blasting against her.

Everything felt numb as she stared at the dark canopy, as pain ebbed and flowed through her, and what she had done rolled up on her.

She had killed a man.

She was sure of it.

Cold chilled her and she tried to fight the darkness as it crowded the corners of her vision, but she wasn't strong enough.

Heavy footfalls shook her awake, had her forcing her eyes open and her hand to her bear spray. She managed to get it off her belt and held it before her in trembling hands as her breath stuttered from her and fear rushed through her again, tearing down what little strength she had left.

Only it wasn't the other man.

The towering man who emerged from the blizzard wasn't one she recognised, although he wore black like the other two had. Maybe he was with them. Maybe she had missed him in Banff when she had noticed the other two. He didn't have a weapon she could see though, or even a flashlight to help him in the dark.

"Stay back." She shook the bear spray at him.

He arched an eyebrow at her, his eyes filled with an unimpressed look as she threatened him. "No need to get violent. I'm only here to help. I heard the gunshots."

She didn't have time to contemplate just how smooth and deep his voice was, or how it seemed to ease the tension from her. Sickness swept through her. *Get violent.* She was deeply aware there was a body near her—a death she had caused. Panic gripped her once more, so tightly this time she felt as if she was going to pass out as she fought for air.

"I killed him," she muttered, her hand shaking hard now, causing the bear spray canister to jitter all over the place. She let it drop to her lap as fatigue washed through her, as the last of her strength left her.

The man looked to his left, strode over to the body and hunkered down next to it. He grabbed the flashlight and used it. She didn't watch him as he inspected the dead man, couldn't bring herself to look at what she had done.

"You killed him if you shot him in the head," he drawled and she felt his gaze on her.

He moved on the edges of her vision as she stared at the sky, struggling to breathe and get her panic under control. She hadn't killed him? For some reason, it wasn't a comfort. She still felt responsible for his death. She had pushed him down the slope, had caused his death.

The man bent and straightened again.

"A handgun?" He looked at her and she still couldn't bring herself to look at him. "Guess he wasn't a hunter then."

He went back to the body and crouched beside it as he checked it over again, didn't seem at all bothered by what he was doing or the fact the man was dead. "Any idea who he was?"

She was in too much shock to speak, could only shake her head.

He looked at her and seemed to notice it.

He went from all business to all softness as he stood and came to her, rounded her and eased to his knees on her left side. The flashlight he gripped illuminated him enough that she could make him out more clearly. His blue eyes locked on her arm, concern flickering in them as he checked the gash in her jacket.

She swallowed and looked up at his face, was sure it was the shock talking, but he was handsome as he smiled at her and dimples formed in his cheeks. Some god had sculpted this man to perfection, with his strong jaw, straight nose and a slight indent in his chin, and blue eyes that were as deep as an ocean.

"You in shock?" His smile faltered, the corners of his mouth turning downwards as his blond eyebrows pinched. "I think you're in shock."

She was sure she was.

She was in tremendous pain, but she couldn't feel it as she stared at him, as she swam in those baby blues.

"Shit," he muttered and pulled his gloves off. He pressed his fingers to her face. "You're freezing. We need to get you somewhere warm."

She was warm.

"The bullet only grazed your arm. You should be good to move. Maybe this whole thing has been a bit too much for you though." He stood and pulled her onto her feet.

She screamed when she placed weight on her left leg, sank to her backside on the cold hard ground and clutched her ankle, breathing through the pain.

"Christ, I'm sorry." He dropped to his knees beside her, gently took hold of her legs and eased them in front of her. She flinched when he moved her left one and he noticed it. "What happened here?"

He felt her leg from her thigh downwards and she tried not to think about where his hands were. When he reached just above her ankle, she clenched her teeth hard and whimpered as fire blazed outwards along her bones.

"Slope. Fell." It was all she could manage.

His blue eyes lifted to the slope behind him.

"Gods, that's a long drop." He glanced at the dead man, a look in his eyes that told her he thought she was damned lucky not to have ended up like him.

He gripped her arm again and eased her onto her feet this time. She tried not to place any weight on her left leg, but even with it all on her right, her ankle still throbbed madly. Her stomach turned and she clutched it, breathed through the nausea as she stood with the man holding her upright.

"I'm not sure you can walk." He cast a worried look at her leg.

"Can." She bit the word out, determined to get away from the dead body and from the other man, sure he was after her by now.

She hobbled a few steps and then stopped when the man didn't follow her and it hit her that she wasn't sure where she was going or what she was doing. The sensible thing to do was get back to her car and get away from this place before she could get this kind man in trouble too.

She almost cursed. Her keys were in her backpack. The backpack she had left behind when the two men had shown up. She couldn't go back for it. By now, the other man would be recovering from receiving a blast of bear spray in his face. He might be waiting for her to return for her things, or for the man who had come after her to bring her back to him so they could leave to meet up with Karl.

She glanced at the man who stood before her. Maybe he had a car she could use.

He stepped up to her, stooped and placed her arm around his shoulders. "Come on."

She hopped along beside him, her right leg trembling, entire body quaking as he led her deeper into the forest, away from the mountain. Where was he taking her? Was it safe to trust him? The sensible side of her said it wasn't, but one glance at him was enough to make the rest of her feel she could. There was something about him that set her at ease and made her feel safe.

Protected.

It was probably just shock talking.

"Do you have a car?" She looked up at him.

He kept his profile to her. "Me? No. My brother has one though. Did you walk all the way up here?"

She shook her head.

He glanced at her. "So you have a car?"

She nodded this time and fought a grimace as a thousand needles jabbed up her left leg. "No keys. In backpack. Lost it."

He huffed. "You're in no state to be driving anyway."

She looked up at him now, trying to see whether she really could trust him, needing to convince the sensible side of her that he wasn't a danger to her. He looked as if he could handle himself and his black jacket hid some serious muscles she could feel as he moved with her, easily helping her walk. He knew this area too, had managed to find her from wherever he had come from, despite the weather.

"Where are we going?" She peered into the forest he illuminated with the flashlight he gripped in his other hand and then at the sky, trying to make out which direction they were heading.

"I'll take you to my place." He noticed it when she tensed, but misinterpreted the reason for it. "I won't hurt you. As soon as you're strong enough to leave, you can go. I'll stay with my brother while you take my cabin."

She hadn't feared he would try anything with her. She feared she was going to pull him into danger.

"What's your name?" Her voice trembled slightly as she asked that.

"Lowe." His tone was gruff, but the sound of his voice still warmed her.

She tried to smile, but it came off as a grimace as her leg ached. "Cameo."

He slid her a look, one that put fire in his blue eyes that burned away all trace of gentleness.

"Whatever trouble you're in, I'll keep you safe, Cameo. I swear it."

CHAPTER 4

Lowe helped Cameo over a particularly rough and uneven patch of ground, holding her gently, careful not to hurt her as she hopped along beside him. Every inch of him was aware of where the slight female pressed against him, how his fingers gripped her ribs beneath her right arm, and how her breath hitched whenever her leg hurt her. The feel of her was driving him crazy, together with the scent of her blood as it swirled around him in the wind, and the fact she had been attacked.

That last one had his bear side wild with a need to rip apart the male who had done this to her, made it uneasy and filled him with a deep desire to tuck her closer to him, sheltering her in his arms.

He had thought the urge to shift and attack that had come over him when he had found her would have faded by now, but it was still going strong, kept him quiet as it filled his mind with images that made him restless. The replay spinning around his head was different every time, but one thing remained constant—the human male had survived the fall and Lowe had been the one to kill him.

Lowe glanced down at Cameo, studying her profile as she stared intently at the ground, carefully picking her way over it.

He wanted to know more about her situation, but one look at her was all it took for him to see she wasn't ready to handle being questioned. She was too pale, her eyes unfocused despite how fiercely she watched the ground before her, and although she was doing her best to hide it from him, she was in pain. In shock.

Talking about the male would only remind her of what she had done. It would only make her condition worse. She wasn't handling it well, was as quiet and lost in thought as he was, and his gut said she was still blaming herself for what had happened.

The scent of fear was still strong on her too, as acrid and overpowering as it had been when he had come upon her, when she had refused to look at the body, and it triggered a powerful reaction in him—a fierce need to protect her.

That urge had him striking out on a south-eastern path rather than heading directly east to attempt to find Knox. The weather was abysmal now and night was closing in, and getting Cameo somewhere warm where she could rest took priority. Knox was going to be furious with him when he returned to Black Ridge, but his brother would return there. He knew it in his heart and it calmed him, eased the need to find him and make sure he was all right.

Knox might understand his reason for choosing not to join up with him again when he met Cameo and saw the state of her. Being out in the cold was only going to worsen her condition, could even prove fatal for her. He knew a little about humans. They were weak, easily succumbed to hypothermia. He feared that her state of shock and her injuries might make it easier for hypothermia to seize her.

She hissed in a breath when she wobbled on a root and was forced to put her left foot down to steady herself.

He glared down at her injured leg. He wasn't sure what was wrong with it, and he wanted to get a good look at it because he feared it might be broken. The need to get her tucked safe and warm inside his cabin grew stronger, rousing an urgency inside him that had his bear growing even more restless and had him turning to her.

"I can carry you." The moment those words left his lips, she turned a glare on him. "I really don't think now is the time to be stubborn."

He pointed the flashlight at her leg, drawing her gaze to it.

"It's fine," she bit out. "I can walk."

He wanted to growl at that, but held it back, aware that if he unleashed it he would only terrify her.

To prove her point, she broke free of his arm and defiantly hobbled a few steps, the toe of her left boot barely touching the dirt before she hopped forwards.

He grunted. "Fine. We'll do this the hard way... but you don't need to be stubborn about it."

"I'm not stubborn," she snapped, fire in her eyes as she scowled over her shoulder at him.

Maybe the shock was passing, for her at least. It felt as if it hit him instead as he stood there staring at her, bewitched by her spit and fire, by how her sky-blue eyes gained a sharp edge. She was beautiful, even when the soft curve of her jaw set in a hard line as her full lips flattened and her cheeks reddened. Caramel-coloured eyebrows knitted hard above those entrancing eyes, ones that dared him to say another word about her being stubborn.

Lowe got the feeling he had been wrong. She wasn't stubborn. She was scared. She didn't want to rely on him any more than she already was, clearly feared that she was pulling him into her mess. She was responsible. Courageous. A female who felt sure she could handle everything on her own.

Only she didn't need to, not anymore.

That look in her eyes said she wouldn't concede easily though, and as she dropped her gaze to her feet and leaned against a tree for support, he recognised something else. She didn't want to be a burden.

Here was a female who was clearly used to being strong and capable, and who was ashamed of what had happened to her. Foolish female. Being injured and relying on someone else didn't make her weak. Refusing help was being weak. Clinging to some crazy notion that she could do it all alone and hurting herself further just to prove a point to herself, well, that was something he wouldn't allow.

He strode up to her, wrapped his right arm around her ribs and gripped her firmly, but not hard enough to accidentally hurt her, showing her that she wasn't going to push him away that easily.

"You want to walk, then we'll walk." He looked down into her eyes and hated the edge of hopelessness and vulnerability they possessed. He sighed. "But, if you want me to pick you up, give you a rest like, just ask, Cameo. I'm not offering to do it to come across as some macho male or dominate you. I'm not trying to trample your independence or make you feel weak and helpless. I'm just trying to stop you from hurting and to help you get through this."

She lowered her gaze to the ground again, a solemn look crossing her face. "I know."

Her eyes slipped shut and she sighed.

Lowe leaned across her and placed the flashlight in her right hand, and she frowned down at it as he closed her gloved fingers around it.

"Light the way for us. We're heading that way." He directed the flashlight towards where he knew Black Ridge to be.

She nodded and clutched the light, kept it steady on the ground just a few feet in front of her, so it illuminated her path, and he started walking with her again. He could feel the tension in her easing as they crawled along at a snail's pace. Giving her something to do that made her feel useful had been the right move. She was far more relaxed now, focused on her task, and was even leaning more heavily on him, using his strength and his support to help her move easily over the uneven terrain.

At this rate, they might make it to his cabin before the month was out.

"You really live up here?" Her soft voice barely reached him as a gust of wind roared through the trees and her question ended on a shriek as it shook snow loose from the trees and it showered down on her.

Lowe released her for a moment and brushed the white powder off the hood and shoulders of her dark jacket, and then slid his arm back around her. "This storm is getting worse."

He scoured the route ahead of him, trying to make out where they were. The snow made it hard for him to recognise anything as it raced through the trees at almost a horizontal as the gale caught it.

"We should find somewhere to stop for the night."

She locked up tight as he said that, her blue eyes leaping to his face. "We can't stop outside in this weather. We'll freeze."

"Wasn't talking about outside." He squinted through the snow and thought he spotted a sheer rocky wall ahead that he recognised. "There's plenty of caves around here."

She gasped. "And plenty of bears or cougars in those caves."

"The local wildlife won't bother us." He chuckled and when she looked at him as if he was insane, he tried to think like a human, because he didn't like her looking at him that way, as if she wanted to run a mile from him. He glanced at her belt. "You've got your trusty bear spray. That'll keep us safe."

She looked as if she wanted to touch it to check it was still there.

He sneered at it in his mind. Infernal shit. He hated that stuff, had wanted to roar at her when she had threatened him with it, his bear side quick to remember every damned time some bastard had sprayed him with it in the past. Humans were often a little too trigger happy when it came to bear spray. Not once had he been a threat to a male or female who had hit him with the fiery, horrific concoction the canister contained.

"We'll need a fire." She was sounding more like she was going to agree to finding a nice sheltered spot to bed down for the night. "I can make one."

"I bet you can, but I think I can handle it just this once." He guided her left, towards the cliff he had seen, and breathed a sigh of relief when it turned out to be the one he had been thinking about.

She froze and refused to move as she spotted the entrance to a small cave, one that was tucked in a bend in the rock, away from the direction of the wind. "What about bears?"

He inhaled, pretending to be getting ready to sigh when he was really scenting the air. "No bears. But I'll check it out."

He released her and went to walk away, but she grabbed his sleeve in a fierce grip. He looked back at her, his gaze colliding with hers as his eyebrows rose high on his forehead to disappear beneath his black hat.

"Won't you need this?" She held the flashlight out to him.

"Oh. Yeah. That'll help." He smiled at her, took the light he didn't need to be able to see in the dark and waggled it. "Silly me."

It was hard remembering to act like a human when he hadn't been around one in so long.

He pretended to use the flashlight, but kept his eyes away from the bright spot on the ground, not wanting to dampen his naturally good vision by looking at it. When he reached the small cave that extended back into the rock a good fifteen feet, he kept it pointed at the entrance, away from the rear of the cave. As he had suspected, no animals were occupying it. There wasn't even a sign one had been using it recently.

Lowe went back to Cameo and handed her the flashlight. "Nothing in there. Come on."

He helped her to the cave, settled her on the dirt inside it and left her for only as long as it took to find something he could use to make a fire. Thankfully, there were some twigs and branches inside the mouth of the cave, sheltered from the storm. They were dry enough to use for a fire. He made one close to the mouth of the cave and got it going, warmed his hands a little on it as he waited for the flames to catch and spread before adding more wood to it. It smoked a little, but it would do.

Lowe eased back into the cave, towards Cameo, and settled on his knees in front of her. She still had a death-grip on the flashlight, was using it to inspect every inch of the cave at least a dozen times.

"You good? Warming up?" He smiled when she looked at him and grimaced when she flashed the damned light right in his face.

"Sorry!" She lowered the beam. "Um, yes. I'm warming up a little."

"That's good." He unzipped his black jacket, removed it and placed it around her shoulders.

"Wait. You need this." She tried to take it off, but he gripped the two sides and held it in place.

"I'm good. I'm warm enough." He was cold, but he could handle it and she couldn't.

Her body was frail compared with his and shock was making her vulnerable to the icy chill in the air. He sank onto his backside in front of her boots and looked at her leg.

"When you're warm enough, I'd like to take a look at that leg." He nodded towards it and her gaze fell there, growing distant again.

When she didn't answer, just remained silent with that lost look in her blue eyes, he tried to think of something to say, something to take her mind off the dead man they had left behind in the woods.

He wanted to question her, was worried by the fact there had been a human up in the valley with a handgun of all things. The dead male hadn't been with Archangel, he had gotten that much from what he had seen, but he was trouble. Lowe had found several IDs on him, all of them likely fake, and no car keys.

Either he had lost them like Cameo had apparently lost hers, or there was someone else in the valley looking for her.

Once he had her comfortable at his cabin, safely inside it, he would ask her about what had happened. For now, he would concentrate on getting her to Black Ridge.

Saint wasn't going to be happy with him when he rolled into the Ridge with Cameo in tow, but Lowe wouldn't take no for an answer about her staying there.

They would just have to be careful while she was at the Ridge and keep their secret under wraps until she was gone. His bear side wanted to moan and roar, grew agitated at the thought of her leaving, and it made him restless, had him looking towards the mouth of the cave as a need to shift came over him.

"Did you hear something?" Cameo whispered.

Lowe shook his head. "Nothing out there. Not even my brother."

"Your brother?" Her gaze drilled into the side of his face. "You mentioned him before. You think he's out there in this storm?"

"I know he is. When I heard the gunshots, I left him on a trail to come find you." And now he was worried about him because the storm was growing worse still and Knox had been a long way from the lodge and home when Lowe had left him.

The gods only knew where his brother was now.

Knox would have come after him, wanting to stick close and protect him. Chances were high that his brother was out there in the woods somewhere, searching for him in this blizzard. He could only hope his brother had enough sense to find somewhere to bed down for the night.

Knox had the advantage over him there. He could shift into his bear form to sleep the night away and wouldn't need a fire to keep him warm. His dense fur would do the job.

Lowe got to freeze his ass off in his human form instead.

"Are you worried about him?"

He looked back at Cameo. "Nah... A little. Knox can handle himself. He'll pick a cave and bed down until the weather passes."

"How long have you lived up here?" Her gaze grew curious.

Lowe shuffled back to face her and started unlacing her left boot. "A while. It's nice up here. Quiet... Normally."

He smiled at her.

She almost smiled back at him, but her gaze dropped to her foot as he pulled her boot off. Her very expensive boot. She had some serious socks on too, and he had noticed her jacket was top of the line. Whoever Cameo was, she was a woman who knew her stuff, who looked almost comfortable out here in the wilderness, as if she belonged here.

Lowe undid the zipper that ran a few inches up the leg of her salopettes from the hem, loosening them, and then gently eased the material up to reveal bare skin.

"Is it bad?" There was a tremble in her voice now.

He shook his head, because he wasn't really sure what he was looking at. There were some nasty bruises on her shin and up her calf, and a few grazes. He removed his gloves and blew on his hands, trying to warm them up. She still tensed and hissed in a breath when he touched her calf.

"Sorry," he muttered with a glance at her.

She shook her head, her lips tightly compressed as her eyes watered. Maybe it hadn't been his cold hands that had caused that reaction in her.

"It hurts?" He looked down at her leg and then back into her eyes.

She nodded this time, sucked down a breath and fisted her right hand in his jacket, gripping it tightly.

Lowe tried to be gentle as he felt his way up to her knee, gauging her reaction. She didn't tense or cry out. He worked his way lower again and the moment he neared her ankle, she yelped and kicked him with her good leg, catching him hard on the chest and knocking him back.

"Oh my God. I'm sorry." Her blue eyes widened in horror as he rubbed at his sternum, clearing a muddy boot print from his checked fleece shirt.

"My fault." He gazed down at her ankle, a frown knitting his eyebrows. "Not sure whether it's a sprain or worse."

"It's a sprain," she said, her voice a little too bright, as if she was trying to make herself believe that, or she could somehow twist fate to make it be a sprain and not a broken bone.

He removed his shirt and her eyes only widened further.

"What are you doing now?" Her gaze darted over his chest as he reached over behind him, gripped the back of his white T-shirt and pulled it off over his head.

"Field dressing." He let the T-shirt fall onto his knees and put his shirt back on, was quick to button it and not only because of the cold. The feel of Cameo's gaze on his bare chest wreaked havoc on him, had him heating to a thousand degrees and his skin feeling too tight. He looked around them and huffed when he realised he had used all the good sturdy wood for the fire. "Binding it will have to do for now. Might help a little."

He tore his T-shirt into two pieces.

"Wait." She sat up straighter and leaned forwards, pulled her gloves off and set them aside. "I'll help. I'm trained in this kind of thing."

"Trained in it?" He flicked a glance at her, lingered as her eyes locked with his and firelight danced over the right side of her face.

Damn, she really was beautiful.

She nodded. "One of the first things I did when I became a ranger."

A ranger.

A lot of things about her suddenly made sense, except the fact there were men after her. That suddenly made a lot less sense for some reason. He couldn't imagine why a park ranger would have armed men chasing after her.

She helped him with the bandage, pretty much took over and did it for him, and stopped just short of admonishing him at one point, which stopped him from pointing out that he didn't have fancy training in the art of field medicine. It didn't stop him from feeling a little less confident around her though.

He took over again when she fought a grimace, rolling the leg of her trousers back down and slipping her boot back on for her.

"Let me take a look at that arm." He jerked his chin towards it and she didn't fight him, shifted his coat from her shoulders and placed it over her legs, and then unzipped her own one.

Lowe moved around to her left side, kneeled and helped her slip her right arm free of the jacket and then eased it down her left one. He placed it over her legs as another layer of warmth and peered at the buff-coloured sweater she wore, one that was pure wool by the look of it. The little ranger really had come prepared, meaning she had known there was a high chance that escaping those men that were after her would end with her trekking through the woods.

He bet that the pack she had lost had everything she could possibly need to survive in the wild in it.

She tensed and looked away when he fingered the slit in her sweater, one that darted across her upper arm. "Is it bad?"

Lowe peered at the wound. "Just a graze. You got lucky. Bullet barely touched you. I'll bandage it to keep the dirt out but it should heal nicely."

The bleak look she gave him said she didn't feel lucky, and when she looked at him like that, as if the weight of the world was on her shoulders and she was too tired to bear it, he wanted to hold her close.

"I swear, Cameo, I'll keep you safe. Nothing… or no one… is going to hurt you while I'm with you."

She swallowed and nodded, her fair eyebrows furrowing as she looked deep into his eyes, reached her right hand up and touched his where it lingered on her left arm. "Thank you, Lowe."

His gaze fell to her lips and then he forced it down to her arm. He busied himself with binding the wound before she could even think about removing her sweater. It was better she stayed in it, and not only because he didn't want her getting colder than she already was. Her proximity was driving him crazy again, had him firmly skirting the edge and feeling desperate for some air as his bear side goaded him, trying to make him give in to his impulses.

It wasn't going to happen.

He had sworn he would keep her safe and not try anything, and he meant to keep that promise.

But her hand lingered on his, the feel of her skin against his too much for him to bear, and for some godsdamned reason he couldn't bring himself to make her stop, to make her take her hand away.

He stared at the bandage on her arm when he had finished tying it, savoured how good it felt to have her touching him, how right it felt.

"Cameo," he started.

Lifted his eyes to hers.

Somehow found the strength to shut down the urges running rampant through him.

"You should get some rest."

Not the words he had wanted to say to her, and not the ones she had wanted to hear judging by how she looked away from him and her cheeks coloured.

He took his hand away from hers, helped her back into her jacket and placed his one over her front to keep her warm. On a long sigh, he twisted and sank onto his backside beside her, coming to rest against the cold wall of the cave.

"I don't think I can sleep," she whispered and glanced towards the mouth of the cave.

He had wanted her to be nearest the fire to keep her warm, but now he could see that had been a mistake. She felt vulnerable being the one closest to the mouth of the cave. He stood and moved around her, eased to his ass on her right side, and looked at her.

"Is that better?" His eyes searched hers, some soft part of him hoping it was.

She nodded and surprised him by resting her head on his arm. Lowe risked it, couldn't deny the urge that ran through him. He lifted his arm and placed it around her shoulders, tucked her against his chest and held her.

Watched over her as she drifted off to sleep.

Keeping his promise to her.

He wouldn't let anything happen to her.

Whoever was after her would have to go through him to get to her.

Even if they brought an army and all the guns in the world. He would protect her until his last breath.

CHAPTER 5

Cameo woke slowly, sleep refusing to release its grip on her. She huddled into the warmth of the jacket wrapped around her and her eyes shot wide open when she realised it wasn't only a jacket draped across her shoulders. Lowe's arm was too. His hand gently gripped her left shoulder, just above where the bullet had caught her, and the shock that rolled through her only grew more intense as she realised something else.

She had been sleeping with her head against his chest. Her heart drummed discordantly to his as it beat against her right ear, picking up pace as she tried to think of something to say. She wasn't sure what to do. She wanted to curse, hoped she hadn't drooled on him, or that he wouldn't make a big deal about the fact she had used him as a pillow.

She wasn't the sort of woman to fall asleep on a man she knew, let alone someone who was practically a stranger to her. Although, Lowe didn't feel like a stranger. Some ridiculous part of her felt as if she already knew him better than she did most of the people she had worked with over the years, and she put it down to shock. The trauma of the last few months had done a real number on her, throwing her into a tailspin where it no longer surprised her that she was acting differently to how she normally would.

"Storm cleared up about an hour ago," Lowe drawled, his deep voice as smooth and sweet as honey to her ears, and holding a rumbling smoky note like whiskey.

He had a voice made for the bedroom.

Cameo showed that stray thought the door. Shock. It was the shock talking.

"How long was I asleep?" She dreaded pulling away from Lowe, and not only because he was warm against her, like a portable radiator that was keeping the chill off her hip and side. She really didn't want to see if she had left a drool patch on his soft, black and green checked shirt.

"I reckon a good nine hours."

"Nine hours?" She jerked away from him, startlingly awake now as her gaze whipped from him to the world outside.

How could she have slept for nine hours? God only knew how close the other man might be to finding her now. She began to wish the storm hadn't cleared up, cursed that clear blue sky she glimpsed through the dark green canopy of the forest. The storm had been hiding their tracks, providing them with cover. Now, the man would be able to spot them from a long distance even through a forest as dense as this one.

"You look worried." And Lowe looked curious, possibly suspicious. "Something I should know about, Cameo?"

She was quick to shake her head. "Nothing. I just... I didn't think I would sleep an hour, let alone nine."

She had honestly thought she had been too wired to sleep, too afraid of what might be out there, whether it was an animal or a human. She looked at Lowe, right into those stunning, rich baby blues, and it hit her that she had been too wired and too afraid to sleep, but then he had placed himself between her and any possible danger, and she had felt safe.

Safer than she had felt in a long time.

In too long.

She couldn't remember the last time she had slept for more than a few hours, and she had the feeling that if Lowe was with her, she could sleep for a day or more, felt so at ease and safe around him that she could easily catch up on all the sleep she had missed since her brother had been killed.

Cameo glanced at the world beyond the mouth of the cave again, dreading going out there while at the same time feeling a pressing need to get moving.

"I'm sensing you want to get out of here." Lowe took his arm from around her shoulders and pushed to his feet, and a strange feeling swept over her.

A chilling sort of coldness that made her want to ask him to hold her again.

This wasn't like her. Capable Cameo, as her work colleagues teasingly called her, didn't rely on others, trod her own path in this world with confidence and certainty. Capable Cameo had been struggling to keep her head above water the last few months though, had been slowly sinking into despair and had been starting to feel that she was going to have to run for the rest of her life or she would be caught.

Killed.

It had taken its toll on her and had worn her down more than she had noticed. Now that she had taken a moment to rest, had found someone she felt she could trust, someone who looked strong enough to help her, it had all rolled up on her and that strength she had thought she possessed was nowhere to be seen.

Lowe bent forwards and offered his hand to her and she stared at it, knew how bleak she looked as his blond eyebrows furrowed, disappearing beneath his black hat, and he gave her a soft look, one filled with understanding and a touch of concern.

He eased to his haunches before her, resting his elbows on his knees, and sighed. "Tough few days, huh?"

She nodded and tried to push it all down inside her, to bottle it up again, but it was all whirling around her head now, images of Nate swirling together with memories of those men when they had come to threaten her, and when she had pushed the one down the slope. She could still hear the sickening crack as he had hit that tree.

"I don't know what you've been through or what you're involved in, Cameo, but I do know you can trust me. Whatever is happening… I can help you. You get to set the rules here though. You want to keep it all to yourself, that's fine. I won't like it, but I'll deal. You want to talk to me about it, you can do that too." Lowe gently placed his hand over hers as she gripped her knees. "You need my help, you've got it."

She stared at him, part of her sure he was an angel, one sent to protect her, because who else would be out here in the middle of nowhere? Who else would offer to help her when he didn't even know the dangerous mess she was caught up in?

As she looked at him, she felt deep in her soul that her luck had changed yesterday. It really had. Some kind deity of fate had put him in her path, right when it had looked as if things were going to get ugly for her and she had reached the end of the line.

Could he really protect her from the destiny she felt awaited her?

She had seen enough movies to know what would happen if Karl got his hands on her, had seen what they had done to her brother. Torture. They would torture her to make her talk, even though she didn't know anything and she certainly didn't have their money. They wouldn't care.

"Hey now." Lowe lifted his hand and brushed his knuckles across her face, startling her.

She blinked and looked at him, shock rolling through her as she felt the cold kiss of tears on her cheeks.

Just great. Now she was crying in front of him. She didn't want to imagine what he was probably thinking as he cleared her tears away, his touch gentle and concern warming his blue eyes. She hated the thought he might be thinking she was weak, another woman who couldn't handle herself, who resorted to breaking down in tears when the going got tough. She wasn't. She lifted her hand, knocking his away as she scrubbed at her face. She was strong. Capable Cameo.

He looked as if he wanted to say something. One half of her imagined it would be something along the lines of telling her that she was allowed to cry because she had been through a lot, and the other half of her imagined it would be some well-intentioned speech about how crying didn't make her weak and that she was strong.

She didn't want to hear either of those things, so she gripped the rough rock wall of the cave and hauled herself onto her feet, grimacing only a little as she dared to put the tiniest amount of weight on her left leg. Pain swept up it in response and she decided against attempting to walk on it.

She was beginning to fear the worst now—it was fractured.

Cameo removed Lowe's black jacket from her shoulders and held it out to him. He looked as if he didn't want to take it, might insist she kept wearing it like a blanket, but then he grabbed it and slipped his arms into it, and zipped it up.

Standing before him like this, she realised just how tall he was. He had a good nine inches on her, maybe more, had to stand at least six-six. He wasn't a slim six-six either. He was a big six-six. Made her feel tiny in comparison. She had met a few men who lived in the wilderness, preferring to keep to themselves and lead a simple life out in the woods, but none of them had been as built as Lowe was. He looked as if he could haul logs without any machinery, could easily fell a tree and drag it to wherever he needed it.

"You hungry?" There was an awkward edge to his eyes as he said that and it dawned on her that it was because she was staring at him. He patted his stomach. "You must be hungry, because I'm ravenous."

He glanced over his shoulder at the cave mouth, lingered looking in that direction. Avoiding her as she continued staring at him, couldn't quite convince herself to stop. Yesterday, she hadn't noticed just how big he was, although she had noticed how handsome he was. She had put that down to shock at the time, but in the cold light of day, he was still as gorgeous as she had thought him when her brain had been addled by pain and fear.

He cleared his throat. "Shouldn't be more than half a day to my cabin. Think you can make it that far?"

Did he mean walking or without food? The thought of trekking half a day wasn't appealing either way. She was hungry, as ravenous as he was, her stomach constantly growling at her for food, and her leg was aching again. She wasn't sure she could hop for half a day, not when hunger was draining what precious strength she had.

Lowe stepped out into the open and she followed him, the thought of trying to walk becoming even less appealing as she saw just how much snow had made it through the forest canopy and settled on the ground.

He cast her a look, one that told her he wanted to say something but he thought she wouldn't like it, and scrubbed his nape, teasing short blond hairs that stuck out from beneath his hat.

"Cameo... I get that... Well, I just think... I know..." He huffed. "I'm going to be blunt. I get you want to walk, but you're going to find it hard going in these conditions with your injury, and I'm really damned hungry and I want to get back to the cabin and get you warmed up before your condition gets worse... so I'm going to carry you, and you can be mad at me all you want about it, but it isn't going to change the fact you're getting carried."

Before she could even form a protest, he stooped and scooped her up into his arms as if she weighed nothing. Damsel in distress wasn't her scene, but the way Lowe's arms tensed against her back and beneath her knees, how gently he held her despite how firm his muscles were against her, and the way it brought their faces close together, felt too good for her to even want to complain and be mad at him.

He stared at her, his lips parting slightly, his gaze holding hers.

After a long silence that felt too comfortable, he muttered something beneath his breath, something she felt sure had been a comment about how she felt pressed against him, and shook his head, as if trying to rouse himself.

Or shake an urge away.

Cameo's gaze fell to his mouth as he started walking and she shook her own head, dislodging the sudden urge that came over her, the tempting thought of kissing him. He might be holding her like a damsel, treating her like a princess, but that didn't mean she had to go all soft over him and start thinking about things like kissing him as if he was some white knight who deserved a token of gratitude from her.

She tucked her hands in her lap, unsure what to do with them, and tried to keep her eyes off him as he walked. As he carried her. It was fine at first, and he was making far quicker progress than they would have had she been trying to walk, but a feeling slowly crept up on her as they left the cave behind and followed the slope downwards into the heart of the valley. She felt awkward, ashamed, like a burden. She had been trained in how to deal with the mountains and she had been so confident in her skills, and part of her felt that this whole affair had only proven how wrong she had been about that, even when the rest knew that even the most experienced ranger wouldn't have been able to deal with what had happened to her.

Cameo glanced at Lowe, that shame eating away at her. He wasn't complaining about carrying her, but he looked strained, his handsome features pinched tightly, and she was sure it was because of her. He needed to rest at least and she needed out of his arms, even if it was only for a moment, until the feeling that she was being a burden and being weak passed.

"Put me down."

He didn't acknowledge her, just kept walking.

She pressed her hands to his chest. "Stop and put me down."

His blue gaze slid to meet hers. "Why?"

"So I can walk. I... You look tired. I'm being a burden." She hated admitting that. Putting it out there only made her feel weak, vulnerable in a way.

He scoffed. "I'm not tired. Not like you weigh anything. You're like a feather."

Soft and easily broken? She knew feathers were really quite strong, but only when they were together, and she was tired and imagined herself as the downy, bendy sort that couldn't hold up to much.

"Put me down." She pressed harder against his chest, tried not to notice just how firm his muscles were beneath her palms and the thick layers of his clothing.

He huffed and scowled at her, but he did put her down. The moment he released her, she wobbled on the slippery ground and was forced to put her left leg down. She gritted her teeth and cried out as pain blazed up her shin, turned her head and made her want to vomit.

"Will you just let me carry you?" Lowe snapped as he caught hold of her arm to keep her upright, his grip strong enough that she could lean into it for support. When she risked a glance at him, his face was as dark as a thundercloud. "Believe me, you aren't a damned burden when you're in my arms, but you're a burden when you're trying to walk. I can't take seeing you in pain."

He slammed his mouth shut.

Cameo stared at him, wide-eyed and stunned by what he had said.

He averted his gaze and refused to look at her again, even when she leaned towards him, trying to see his eyes, needing to see in them what he had meant by that outburst. She had figured him for a gentle man, despite his size and appearance, but even the more sensitive men she had known had never reacted as fiercely as he had to the sight of her in pain. Being a ranger had its perils, and more than once she had been hurt in the field, suffering the odd sprain here and the occasional cut there. The men she had been assigned to work with had fussed over her a little, had helped her out so she wouldn't hurt as much, but not a single one of them had looked ready to pull rank on her or demanded she let them carry her as Lowe had.

None of them had looked furious all because they could see how much pain she was in.

Lowe finally looked at her, and the fury was still there in his blue eyes, a striking need to take care of her that some part of her felt she should find unnerving, maybe even belittling, but the majority of her found oddly appealing.

She nodded and he was quick to scoop her back up into his arms. He turned his profile to her as he started walking again, a troubled edge to his blue eyes that had nothing to do with navigating the treacherous terrain. He didn't like what he had said to her. Had it made him feel vulnerable? Open to her lashing out at him? Or maybe he was worried she would fear him because he had revealed how deeply he wanted to take care of her?

She wasn't afraid of him.

He was as large as a mountain and as rugged as stone, and one look at him was all it took to see he could handle himself, but he was gentle and caring too. Kind. He didn't know her, yet he wanted to take care of her and was helping her. Without him, she was sure she would have died out in the forest, whether it was from cold, an animal attack or the other man finding her.

The other man.

Cameo gazed up at Lowe as he carried her, a thought forming in her mind, one she tried to push out of her head but one that insisted on remaining, lingering, demanding she hear it. He had told her he would help her. If she asked him to help her with her problem, would he do it?

She wanted to believe that he would and that he could handle her trouble for her, but then she remembered that Karl was coming. What if Karl knew about her last location and came here? He wouldn't come alone. He would come with a few of his men at the very least. The thought of Lowe facing off against one man was worrying enough. The thought of him facing half a dozen turned her stomach.

So, no, as much as she wanted to ask him to help her, she couldn't. She didn't want to get him into trouble, feared that she would only end up getting him killed. Her initial plan was the one she would stick with.

She would deal with this alone.

She turned her cheek to Lowe and leaned her head against his broad shoulder, her thoughts weighing her down, pulling a startling reaction from her. She didn't want to leave Lowe, and she wasn't sure it was just fear or pain talking. She had the terrible feeling she was starting to like him.

So she was going to do the right thing.

As soon as she was able, she was going to leave.

And she would probably never see him again.

CHAPTER 6

"You're awful quiet. You fallen asleep?"

Cameo heard the 'again' in that question and roused herself from her heavy thoughts. She tilted her head back. Her gaze collided with Lowe's as he looked down at her, his head angled towards her.

"I'm awake." She felt a little silly saying that when he could see it, was staring down into her eyes, his blue ones warm with concern. "Just a little hungry."

Blaming hunger for her silence was better than admitting that she had spent the last mile or so worrying about what came next, worrying about Karl finding her while she was with Lowe, and worrying about how things might go if that did happen.

"Not far now." Lowe's deep voice rolled over her, calming her turbulent mind.

She wanted to rest her cheek against his shoulder and tell him to keep talking to her, to take her mind off the thoughts that plagued her, and the visions of terrible things playing out in her head. She fell silent again instead and just stared up at him as he walked with her, turning his profile to her as he picked his way through the woods.

"You're not very talkative either," she murmured, hoping to get him to speak to her.

He shrugged, shifting her in his arms. "Worried about Knox."

"The storm cleared up. Maybe he's already back at the cabin." She smiled when Lowe glanced at her, wanting to reassure him and lift his spirits, hoping that if she could brighten his mood it might be infectious and hers might brighten too.

"Maybe." He huffed, smiled that killer smile that caused dimples in his cheeks, and slightly shook his head. "He'll tear me a new one if he is. Suppose I should be prepared for that."

"Because you came to rescue me." She didn't mean those words to come out sullen, but they did. Not only was she being a burden on Lowe, she had separated him from his brother in the middle of a dangerous storm. She almost cursed. If anything had happened to Knox, well, she wasn't sure what she would do, but she knew she would feel responsible.

"Hey, don't give me that look. Knox is tough as nails. He's stronger than a storm, stubborn too. He probably made it back home in the thick of it last night."

She gave a little shrug, trying to shift the weight from her shoulders. "You're the older of the two of you."

"What makes you say that?" He glanced at her, a curious edge to his gaze.

She looked down at her lap as she thought about Nate. "I know the tone. My younger brother was the wild one, and I'm the responsible one. I think I used that tone when talking about him more times than I can count. I always talked about him like he was strong, invincible."

Lowe flexed his fingers against her knee and ribs, was quiet for a moment before he said, "You're talking about him in past tense… You lost him?"

She nodded, sniffed to hold back the tears, and picked at the scuffed knee of her trousers.

"A long time ago?"

She shook her head this time. Lowe held her a little closer and lifted her higher, and her head fell against his shoulder. She sighed, couldn't hold it back as she thought about Nate, as she tried to remember the better days when they had been growing up, when everything had been laughter and the occasional falling out with each other.

When the days had felt as if they wouldn't end and they would always be together.

"There were a few years between us, and it showed at times. Nate always pushed his luck. He was reckless. Crazy at times. He made a lot of mistakes." She smiled slightly as she remembered the funnier ones, the ones that had made her mad but had really been harmless. She had overreacted a lot of the time, but she had always had a deeply protective streak where her kid brother had been concerned.

"You strike me as the cautious, always have a plan type." When Lowe said that, she angled her head back and frowned up at him. He glanced at her, and then his eyes darted back to her and held an apology. "I don't mean it like it's a bad thing. Hell, out of me and Knox, I think I'm the one who prefers to be in control of any situation. Knox is... Well, at times he's the sort to light a fire just to watch shit burn."

She chuckled at that. "He sounds like a handful. Is the age gap between you big?"

"It's huge." He gave her a deadly serious look. "A whole... fourteen minutes."

Her eyes widened. "You're twins?"

He nodded and shrugged again. "Knox likes to act like the big brother at times, but I'm older than him. He says I muscled him out of the way and he was meant to come out first."

She smiled, her mood lightening as she tried to imagine another Lowe, a reckless and wild one. She just couldn't picture it. Lowe had proven himself capable and caring, didn't strike her as the sort who would start a fire of any sort without it being very controlled and unlikely to spread.

"Are you identical twins?" She studied his face—a face made for Hollywood. She could only imagine how devastating Lowe and Knox were on the local women whenever they rolled into town together.

He slid her a teasing look. "I can hear those cogs whirring in that pretty head of yours."

Pretty?

He continued before she could pick him up on the fact he had called her pretty. "We're identical on the outside, but it's a different matter on the inside. He's like our father, and I turned out more like Mom. Knox's hair is darker too, more like Dad's."

Cameo settled against his chest again. Twins. She had never met twins before. Just how different was Knox to Lowe? She bet they were more alike than either wanted to admit.

"Your parents must have had fun raising you." She thought about her own parents. "Mom always said I was the easiest kid anyone had ever had to raise. Whenever Nate did something dangerous, she always used to tell him that she had thought he was going to come out like me, and if she had known she'd have a hellion for a second child, she would have made Dad get the snip. It was just her protective side coming out as anger, but he'd sulk for days and swear he'd change and be better."

"But he never did."

She glanced up at Lowe and shook her head. "No, he never did. As soon as she calmed down, he was back at his old tricks, trying to kill himself on skateboards or snowboarding, or off getting into trouble with the local police."

Lowe gave her a look that said he wanted to ask what had happened to her brother, so she dropped her gaze to her lap and avoided him.

The trees began to thin and Lowe lifted his head.

"And here we are."

Those words made her look up too and her eyes widened as she stared into an enormous clearing blanketed with snow.

A clearing that didn't have just one or two cabins as she had expected. There had to be close to a dozen of them, with five of them near to her and others dotted around beside the forest where it started again directly across from her. None of these cabins had been on her map. What kind of secret life were the people who lived here leading? And there were people who lived here. The cabin that stood proud in the middle of the clearing to her right had smoke curling from the chimney, rising into the cold, still air.

Lowe carried her in that direction, skirting along the edge of the woods, towards a pair of cabins that stood with their backs to the trees. Both of them had a single storey below the steep pitched roof and both were raised on pylons, lifted away from the ground. They were identical, although one was older.

They had to be Lowe and Knox's homes.

"I still can't believe you live up here in winter." She stared at the cabins ahead of her and then peered over his shoulder towards a pair that had been built a short distance away, facing the lone cabin that stood in the middle of the clearing. "How many people live here?"

"Three all year. Five most of the time. Sometimes the others come and stay a little while, but mostly it's the five of us." He rounded the raised deck of the first cabin with its back to the woods and carried her up the steps. "This is me."

He set her down by one of the posts that stood on either side of the steps, supporting the overhanging roof. She gripped the wooden railing beside it and stared out at the settlement, still unable to believe there could be so many cabins in one area without anyone marking it on a map.

Cameo's gaze tracked over the cabin in the centre and drifted towards the woods to her right, trees that it faced, and then backtracked as it caught on something in the deep snow.

"Is that... *blood?*" She stared at the patch of crimson on the trampled snow.

Lowe was quick to turn and even quicker to leap from the deck, landing in the deep snow. He sprinted through it, kicking it everywhere, and her eyes widened further as she spotted something else.

A brown mound of fur in the middle of the huge patch of blood.

A bear.

Lowe was running right for it.

"Oh my God. Don't go near that bear!" She hobbled for the steps, fumbling for her bear spray, her heart a jackhammer against her ribs.

Lowe skidded to a halt a short distance from the injured animal, his back to her.

She missed what he said, the distance between them too great for her to hear him, and limped closer, determined to protect Lowe.

When she was halfway to him, he spoke again, and she caught what he said this time.

"I need to move him."

"It's a bear. You need to back away. I don't know what attacked him, but—" Cameo tried to take another step towards him as she readied her bear spray and grunted when pain shot up her leg. She doubled over, clutching her left knee and breathing through the need to vomit.

Lowe huffed as he pivoted to face her. "Let's get you to my cabin. All nice and toasty like. I'll deal with him, and then I'll deal with those fucking cougars."

He strode to her, swept her up into his arms and carried her away from the bear.

"You can't shoot cougars!" She glared at him, anger getting the better of her as she thought about him hunting down a creature that had only been acting on instinct, doing what it had to in order to survive. "Regulations state that you need a licence for a start. Do you have a licence?"

She hoped to God he didn't. While she knew that maintaining the population of predators was important, she never had been able to stomach trophy hunting, and he sounded as if he was talking about taking out more than just one cat.

"I didn't say I was going to shoot them." Lowe set her down just long enough to open the door to the cabin and picked her up again, carried her inside without removing his boots.

She stared at the trail of snow he left in his wake as he banked right, sweeping between an old dark blue couch and the small kitchen that faced the deck. He carefully carried her up a set of winding wooden stairs. A window came into view and she looked out of it, trying to see the bear, hoping it was gone, scared away by Lowe approaching it. She couldn't see far enough to the right to spot whether it had gone.

Lowe gently set her down on the double bed that took up a lot of the loft bedroom and eased back from her. "Stay here. I'll be back before you know it."

She lunged for his hand and grabbed it, stopping him from leaving.

When he looked back at her, she offered her bear spray. "At least take this."

He curled a lip at the red canister. "I don't need it. The bear is in no condition to fight."

She didn't believe that for a second. Wounded animals were dangerous, liable to attack anyone who approached them. She stared up at him, a tight feeling growing in her chest as she thought about him out there with the bear. Sickness brewed as she searched his eyes, hoping he wasn't one of those men who thought they could befriend wild animals. She knew all the tales of men who had thought that, who had tried to live with bears as if they were pets, and all of them ended badly.

"What's that look for?" His expression softened and he eased to a crouch before her. "Worried about me?"

"Worried you're one of those crazy folks who think befriending bears is going to end well for them." She couldn't stop herself from saying that, needed to hear him say that he wasn't and she was overreacting.

He chuckled, lifted his gloved hand and frowned at it. He pulled his gloves off and brushed his fingers across her cheek.

"You don't have to worry about me. I'm not the crazy one, remember? I'll just run the bear off." He swept his fingers lower, his touch like black magic, soothing her. Or maybe that was his words at work and that earnest look in his eyes that made her feel he hated upsetting her. He stood and turned away from her. "The bear is probably dead anyway. You saw all the blood."

She had. There had been so much of it. She had come across plenty of dead animals in the past, and the brutality of some of the scenes had stayed with her, but she had never seen as much blood as what was out there painting the snow crimson.

Something crossed his face and he hurried down to the ground floor of the cabin. For a moment, she thought he was going to leave, but then she heard him opening and closing cupboards and muttering. He appeared with several colourful bags tucked in his arm and dumped them on the bed.

"To take the edge off." He cast her a smile and she wanted to pick him up on the fact he thought she needed half a dozen bags of chips to merely take the edge off her hunger. He didn't give her a chance. He gave her another serious look. "I'll be back to make something better. Just stay inside, get some rest."

He didn't stick around for an answer, took the winding wooden steps down to the ground floor two at a time and slammed the door behind him.

Cameo stood on wobbling legs and peered out of the window, watched him hurrying across the snow in the direction of the other cabin, and disappear from view.

She sank onto her backside again, grimacing as her leg throbbed, and tried not to worry about Lowe. Her gaze slid to the staircase as the minutes ticked past, thoughts about attempting to head down it and outside to check on Lowe multiplying rapidly.

Sense told her to remain where she was though. Her leg wasn't strong enough for her to make it down the winding steps. She wasn't strong enough. Hunger gnawed at her stomach now, made her head spin from time to time. If she tried to go downstairs, she would only fall and injure herself worse. It was better she stayed sitting on the bed, comfortable and safe. She kept telling herself that, but it didn't stop the need to see Lowe.

Cameo busied herself by removing her green jacket and placing it beside her on the blue covers of the bed, close to a thick fur. She inspected the strip of T-shirt that bandaged her arm, grimacing at the dried patch of blood on the white material and the trail of it down the sleeve of her cream sweater, and then lifted her hand and pulled her woollen hat off. She twisted it in her hands as she waited, aching for Lowe to come back, needing to see that he was safe.

She checked her watch. If he didn't come back in twenty minutes, she was going to tackle the stairs, because she would probably go mad with worry if she didn't.

She closed her eyes and flopped back onto the bed, breathed slowly and evenly in an attempt to calm her racing heart and steady her nerves. They refused to settle as images of bloodstained snow and that bear filled her mind. Worry ate away at her, fear that Lowe was going to get himself killed, fear that her being here was going to get him killed.

Because she felt sure that the one who had shot the bear was the man who was after her.

CHAPTER 7

Lowe was loath to leave Cameo alone in his cabin and was worried that she was going to get ideas about coming after him with that infernal bear spray she was so attached to. The last thing he needed was her seeing him moving a six-hundred-pound grizzly bear into a cabin of all things. His only hope was that his plan to deter her from attempting to come after him by placing her upstairs in his loft bedroom would work and that her dominant sensible side would take one look at the tight, twisting staircase and tell her to keep her ass planted on his bed and wait for him.

Gods, just the thought of her on his bed had his mind racing and heart thundering. He shut down rogue thoughts of how beautiful she was, how good she had felt in his arms, and how badly he had wanted to kiss her back there in the woods, and focused on his task.

Fixing up his alpha.

He wasn't sure what had happened while he was away, but both he and Knox had been wrong—Saint hadn't been safe in the storm.

Or maybe he had, and the clear weather was to blame for the state of Saint and the fact he couldn't sense the female cougar anywhere on the property.

The brothers had come to take her back, which explained the blood and his beat-up alpha, and might even explain why Saint was lying in the snow just staring in the direction of Cougar Creek and showing zero intention of moving.

Lowe reached his side and looked him over, worry cutting him deep as he saw all the lacerations through Saint's thick brown fur and took in all the blood. How long had Saint been lying out in the cold, bleeding to death? He didn't want to think about what might have happened if he hadn't come back, shook it away before it could take hold because he was here now, and he was going to take care of Saint and make sure he survived to fight another day.

A fight Lowe feared might be for the female cougar.

Lowe had had his heart broken enough times to know the look on Saint's face, even when he was in his bear form. He could practically feel how miserable his alpha was, could see in his dark eyes that he was a shell of the male Lowe had left behind when he and Knox had headed out.

The big bear was missing the cougar.

Clearly wanted her back.

Well, lying in the snow wasn't going to make that happen.

Saint's eyes slipped shut.

Panic lanced Lowe's heart.

"Come on, now. No time to sleep." Lowe sucked in a sharp breath as he eased to a crouch on Saint's right and reached for the deep wound on his shoulder.

Saint growled and weakly bared fangs at him, a sign of life that was both a relief and had his worry increasing. Just how close to death was Saint?

Lowe edged his hand back, couldn't keep the bite from his tone as concern got the better of him, the thought that Saint just wanted to let himself bleed out angering him. "Fine. I'll give you a pass for now. But you need to move. Got it?"

Saint grunted and kept staring at the trees.

Lowe huffed and stood. "Don't make this easy on me or anything. When I hurt you, remember it's your own damned fault."

He looked around the clearing, trying to figure out how to get Saint out of the cold. Warming him up was a priority. The cold would be sapping what little strength Saint had left. His injuries would already be healing, but Lowe would deal with those too. Of course, it would be easier if Saint would just shift back.

Lowe stomped towards Saint's cabin.

He had the feeling that Saint didn't want to shift back though, even though he was clearly in pain. Normally, intense pain caused them to shift back to their human forms, which meant Saint had to be holding on to his bear form. Lowe suspected he knew why. In their bear forms, emotions were weaker, overshadowed by animal instincts. All the little feelings he had in his human form boiled down to only a few when he was a bear.

Lowe had shifted once or twice after getting his heart broken, using his bear side to escape the pain of his feelings.

He took the steps up to Saint's cabin and walked inside, heading between the log burner on the left and the couch that stood in the middle of the cosy home. Or at least a home that should be cosy. He paused and tossed some firewood into the burner, stoked it a little until it was going again, and then continued with his mission.

Operation Drag-a-Bear.

He found what he was looking for in the cupboard at the far end of the room, gripped the climbing rope and tugged hard, testing its strength. It was old now, but it seemed strong enough to do the job.

Lowe headed back outside to Saint, canted his head and tried to figure out how to do this. He wished Knox were here. With the two of them, the rope wouldn't be necessary. They could each grab a leg and just pull Saint.

It was just him though. He couldn't scent his brother in the area, couldn't feel him either. He glanced over his right shoulder, beyond Saint's cabin to the head of the valley, worry about his alpha turning to worry about his brother. Was Knox out there still, looking for him? Gods, he hoped his brother wasn't in trouble.

He pulled down a breath, told himself that Knox would be fine, and vowed that if he hadn't returned by the time he had Saint comfortable and healing up nicely, he would head out and look for him.

Lowe bent and grabbed Saint's left hip, fisting his dense fur, and lifted it. He shoved the end of the rope under his belly and then set him down, moved to his right hip and hauled it up. He fumbled around beneath Saint, ignoring his groaning growls and moans of protest, reaching blindly for the end of the rope. He smiled when he found it, gripped it tightly and tugged, threading the rope under his alpha.

He twisted the two strands of the rope together into one, sucked down a deep breath to gather his strength and tugged on it. Saint growled as he slid backwards, the rope biting into his sides.

"At least the snow makes some things easier," Lowe grunted and turned, set the rope over his right shoulder and hauled Saint towards the cabin.

Saint didn't fight him, which was one thing he had going in his favour. Lowe fought to keep his footing on the compacted snow, digging his heels in with each step so he didn't fall flat on his face every time he tugged Saint forwards. When they reached the steps, Lowe turned back to face the bear, gripped the rope in both hands and yanked him up the first step and then the next one.

When Saint's head hit the bottom step, he snarled and grunted and began fighting Lowe. It was a weak attempt at escape, one that spoke of how tired Saint was. Lowe held on to the rope, refusing to let Saint have his way, dragging him up onto the deck.

Lowe reached the door and released the rope, huffed as he looked at Saint's round backside and the gap he had to pull it through, and then at the interior of the cabin.

"Should've moved the damned furniture earlier." He swiped the back of his hand across his forehead, clearing the sweat away, and went into the cabin.

He kept his senses pinned on Saint so he couldn't make a break for it as he moved the couch out of the way, clearing enough room in front of the log burner, and then went back to him.

"Getting your fat ass into this cabin is going to hurt. Just remember… it's your own damned fault." Lowe grabbed the rope and began tugging.

Saint growled and groaned as Lowe hauled him backwards, as his rear got stuck in the doorway and Lowe had to brace his left foot against the frame for leverage. The big bear pushed onto his back feet and shuffled forwards, his weakest attempt at escape yet. He ended up flat on his stomach, stretched out long before Lowe.

"Thought that would get you moving." Lowe grinned and wanted to congratulate himself on making this whole thing a lot easier for him.

Saint didn't respond, just sank against the wooden boards of the deck and went far too still for Lowe's liking.

Lowe gripped his hind legs, pulling them out behind him, and shook him. "Don't sleep now, buddy. Rise and shine."

Saint moaned at him, the low rumbling groan sounding mournful. Yeah, Lowe had been there. He had been there more times than he wanted to admit, and he had thought he had learned his lesson, but his gaze strayed to his right, his mind fixed on a point a few hundred feet beyond the thick log wall that blocked his view.

Cameo was beautiful, smelled like heaven, and fit against him so perfectly that all he wanted to do for the rest of his life was hold her in his arms.

Part of him warned that no good would come of this, while the rest ached to see her again.

"What's gotten you so down anyway? So the cougars took the female back. You should have known it would happen." Lowe shoved thoughts of Cameo out of his head and hauled Saint backwards into the cabin.

Saint responded to that by digging his five-inch-long front claws into the wood, splintering it as he tried to anchor himself and stop Lowe from pulling him. It was just as Lowe had suspected then. His alpha had fallen for the female, was miserable without her, and thought it was all over.

Lowe sighed. Some females were worth fighting for and he had the feeling this female was one of them, and so was Cameo.

He pulled Saint in front of the fire and the big bear lay there, his front and hind legs stretched out on the wooden floorboards.

"You look like a fucking rug." Lowe stepped over him and went to a cupboard near the stairs, rifled around the shelves and found what he was looking for.

He grabbed the large black bag, went back to Saint and set it down near his head. Saint bared fangs at him, a pathetic attempt to warn him away that Lowe wasn't going to heed.

"Yeah, I'm about to let you bleed out. I don't think so." Lowe pulled bottles and bandages from the bag and scowled at him, at all that thick, coarse brown fur that stood between him and Saint's injuries. "You could make this a lot easier on both of us by shifting back."

But that feeling struck him again, the one that said Saint was staying in his bear form because it was easier to handle the hurt that way. It wasn't like Saint to be like this. Lowe couldn't remember ever seeing him caught up in a female.

Lowe tended to his shoulder as best he could, cleaning the wound and mopping up the blood with towels. He was almost done with the first of Saint's injuries when the bear suddenly decided to move, almost knocked Lowe on his ass as he tried to stand. Lowe grabbed him and shoved him back down, making him stay.

"Now you get feisty?" Lowe huffed and went back to tending to his wound, secretly relishing the stronger sign of life from Saint. Maybe his alpha was going to be all right after all. Maybe there was still enough fight left in him for him to make it through his heartache and find the strength not to let the female get away from him. "Just lay there and accept your fate."

He worked to clean the next wound, losing himself in the task, trying to keep his thoughts off Cameo. His heart wanted to think about her though. He needed a distraction, a better one than saving his half-dead alpha apparently.

Movement behind him had him stiffening, fearing that it was Cameo and she had left the safety of his home and snuck up on him while he had been focused on Saint. But it wasn't her soft scent that hit him.

It was a masculine one.

"Christ! What happened to him?"

Lowe had never been so relieved to hear his twin's voice as Knox stepped into the room and sank to his knees beside him on the wooden floorboards.

Lowe flinched in time with Saint as he dabbed at the wound on the bear's right shoulder, cleaning the last of the deep grooves in his flesh. "I came back and found him out in the snow like this. Don't know how long he was out there, but I do know it was the cougars. The female is gone. Place reeks of them."

"I'll murder them." Knox's voice lost its sharp edge as he looked back over his shoulder into the clearing. "Gods, look at all that blood. You think it's all his?"

Lowe nodded and looked at Knox, tried to keep all their spirits up as he said, "He'll be fine."

He didn't really believe that and the look on Knox's face said he didn't either.

"I was about to kick your ass for running off like that, but now… I'll save it for later." Knox ran a shaky hand over his dark blond hair, mussing it. "I don't want to think about what would have happened if you hadn't come back here. Someone needs to put those cougars down."

Lowe slid a look at his brother, worry arrowing through him. "No one is going off to start a war. Saint needs us here."

"Why didn't he just shift back and come inside?" Knox eyed the wound and then Lowe. "Wound like that is painful, sure, but no reason to lay out in the snow waiting for help."

Lowe gave him a look, one he knew had conveyed his suspicions when Knox's expression only grew darker and more grim.

Saint hadn't been waiting for help.

He had been waiting for the cougar female to come back.

Or death to take him.

Knox huffed, grabbed one of the clean towels, and stood. He went to Saint's rear and started drying his fur and massaging his legs, warming him up. His brother was right. Saint might want to give up, but they couldn't, and they wouldn't let him either. They would get him healed and then they would convince him to follow his heart and fight for the female.

Or at least Lowe would convince him.

Knox would probably try to make Saint do the opposite, giving up on the female and forgetting her.

It was growing dark by the time Lowe had finished cleaning all of Saint's wounds and he couldn't stop himself from glancing at the door every few seconds.

"You got somewhere you need to be?" Knox said as he watched him from the other side of Saint.

Lowe avoided his gaze, dropping it back to his work, even though he had no work left. Every single one of Saint's wounds were clean and now on the mend, and Knox had dried him. A heavy silence fell as Saint dropped off to sleep, as Lowe sat there with his brother staring at him.

"I know you have a visitor in your cabin." Knox didn't sound happy about it either, and Lowe braced himself, sure that his brother was going to tell him to get rid of her or lecture him on the dangers of having a human at the Ridge and then tell him to get rid of her. Only his brother just heaved a long sigh and scrubbed a hand over his hair. His stormy blue eyes dropped to Saint. "I'll keep an eye on him. You go get some rest."

That surprised him and he glanced at Knox, his gaze colliding with his, and wasn't sure what to say.

"Don't give me that look, like you're shocked I have a soft bone in my body." Knox grabbed one of the towels and tossed it at him, hitting him hard in the face. It smelled like wet bear. "You might want to make a break for it before I change my mind."

Lowe eased onto his feet, grimacing as his stiff muscles ached, and turned for the door.

Knox stopped him with only a handful of words.

"You have until morning, and then I want to meet her… and you know Saint will too."

CHAPTER 8

Lowe kept his head down as he stepped out of Saint's cabin, stared at his boots as he banked right at the bottom of the steps and headed for his own home across the compacted snow, troubled by the thought of Knox meeting Cameo, let alone the thought of Saint meeting her. His alpha wasn't going to be happy about her presence at the Ridge, and he really wasn't going to be happy when he learned that she had seen him in his bear form.

Although part of him felt sure Saint already knew about that.

It wasn't as if the big bear had been unconscious when Lowe had approached him, and Cameo had been loud when she had called out to him, warning him away from Saint.

An electric shiver chased down his spine, heat rolling through his tired muscles in its wake, and he lifted his head and pinned his gaze on the slender, human female standing on his deck, one gloved hand gripping the railing that ran around it and the other clutching the can of bear spray.

He looked back over his shoulder in the direction of Saint's cabin and then hurried to her, his heart picking up pace, and not because of the sight of her. Slim moonlight highlighted her face, making her look too pale, but even more beautiful at the same time. She wore her coat, but her hat was gone, revealing loose silky waves that had him thinking about how it would feel to sink his hand into them and grip them as he kissed her.

Lowe kicked that urge aside and focused on the problem he potentially had.

"How long have you been freezing your ass off on my deck?" He eyed her closely, trying to read the answer in her blue eyes.

Her dark eyebrows furrowed as she looked from him to Saint's cabin and back again. "I was worried. It's been hours. I was going to come and find you, but then I saw someone out here. I saw him go to that cabin."

She pointed the bear spray at it.

Lowe scowled at the canister, his bear side pushing him to step aside, out of the line of fire. "It was my brother. I'm sorry I was gone so long."

He glanced past her at his cabin. A cabin that now had a soft glow emanating from inside it and smoke curling from the metal chimney. Cameo had been busy since he had left her. Trying to fill the time and take her mind off the fact he had gone off to deal with a potentially deadly bear? He looked back at her, right into her eyes, and caught the worry in them, and the fatigue, and maybe a hint of relief too.

Lowe lifted his hand and went to run it around the back of his neck, grimaced as he smelled Saint's blood on it and dropped it to his side. He mounted the steps to the deck, stopping one down from Cameo. Even then, she was shorter than him, barely reached his chin. The urge to tuck her to his chest and hold her was strong, but he resisted it and focused on dreaming up a reasonable explanation for his absence since she hadn't seen anything.

"Saint got hurt running animals off the property and I had to take care of him." Lowe wanted to growl at the thought of Saint having to fight the cougars alone, knew in his gut that it hadn't been just one of them that had shown up to take the female back.

Saint would have faced all the brothers.

"Saint? Is that a dog or man? Please tell me it isn't that bear, because I've seen how this sort of thing—"

"It's a man." Lowe cut her off before she could slip into another rant about how dangerous it was to befriend bears. "Runs this place. It's his property."

"Is he going to be all right?" She looked genuinely worried now, glanced at the blood on his hands as her brow furrowed.

Lowe nodded. "Knox is taking care of him, but I'll probably have to lend a hand at some point. Come on, let's get you back inside and warmed up."

He stepped up onto the deck, thought about taking her arm and then swept his bloodstained hand out towards the door instead. He didn't think she would appreciate him rubbing blood all over her jacket.

She hopped towards the door and eased it open, and he wanted to groan as warmth swept around him, ached to sink into that heat and sleep for a few days, maybe a couple of months.

"Like it tropical?" He grinned at her back.

She was probably burning through half his store of wood to keep the temperature in the cabin so high.

She grimaced as she glanced back at him. "I think I got carried away. I was a bit cold."

"We'll leave the door open a while." The fierce heat might do him a favour and melt the snow around his cabin.

He raked his gaze down Cameo's curves, his temperature soaring higher. Who needed a fire to keep warm when he had a female like Cameo near him? It wasn't just her figure that inflamed him and drew him to her, it was her personality too. She was strong, and despite what she might think about herself at the moment, she was the most capable female he had ever known. Probably the most sensible female too.

He followed her inside, the log burner like a furnace to his left as he entered, and removed his jacket, hanging it on the peg just behind the door. Cameo removed hers too and held it, tossed another furtive glance at the door as she continued to grip the bear spray as if her life depended on it.

"What about the bear?" she whispered with a glance at him now.

Lowe stepped past the coat rack to the kitchen and looked out of the window as he washed his hands, using some of his store of water to rinse the blood off them. "Gone. Won't be seeing that bear again. It must have spooked when we approached it."

"It's not dead?" The note of fear in her voice made him look at her and flooded him with an urge to hold her.

He dried his hands instead, trying to keep his cool. He didn't like lying to her, but it wasn't as if he could tell her the truth. Besides, he had the feeling he wasn't the only one omitting the truth here and there.

"Probably dead by now. It was in bad shape. You saw it." He tossed the towel onto the small patch of counter near the sink and held his hand out to Cameo.

When she didn't pass her coat to him, just hugged it tighter, he crossed the short span of wooden floorboards between them and took it from her. He clutched it in his left hand and lifted his right one, couldn't stop himself from brushing his fingers across her pale cheek and into the spun silk of her hair. The tips of it were gold, but it faded to honey and then brown at the roots.

"What?" She raised her hand and it brushed his as she reached for her hair, sending a thousand volts shooting up his arm.

"Just… not seen hair like yours before." He felt like a bit of a dolt having to confess that, and for staring at it so intently.

"Oh." She fidgeted with a thick strand of it. "I… I don't normally… It's usually just brown. I was in Vancouver a few months ago and did it on a whim."

He smiled at the way she said that, as if doing something on a whim was a terrible thing, but then it was probably very unlike her. He had the feeling that normally a decision like getting her hair done would have involved numerous days of debating styles and colours and doing research.

Lowe hung her coat on a peg and helped her to the navy couch that stood at an angle in the middle of the living space, facing the log burner in the corner of the room. She sank onto it, her breath leaving her on a weary sigh, and leaned forwards, reaching for her boots. He eased to his knees before her and unlaced them, gently slipped them off her feet and stood.

"Better?" He carried the boots to the door and placed them on the mat to the right of it, near the log burner, and removed his own boots and set them next to hers.

Tried not to think about how good they looked together.

Or the fact he had never had female company in his cabin before.

"Much." That single word held a lot of pain.

Lowe looked over his shoulder at her, turned and frowned when he caught her trying to unzip the leg of her black salopettes. He strode back to her and sank to his knees on the fur rug again.

"Here, let me." Because just the sound of her in pain was enough to drive him wild with a need to take care of her, to ease her and stop her from hurting.

Something about this female had bewitched him. Maybe she wasn't human. Witches smelled human. Although, he doubted a witch would be a park ranger. Not glamourous enough for them. Light witches loved nature, but probably not enough to work in the parks, taking care of the land. All the witches he had met had preferred living on their own patch of land and making money off spells and elixirs made from the flowers, herbs and plants they grew.

There was a witch near Golden who had been slowly expanding her property with the income she made from selling love potions and other tonics and now owned acres in the valley, including a large area of forest.

Going to see her hadn't been Lowe's finest hour but he had managed to stop himself from buying a potion that would make the object of his affection at the time love him back.

He focused back on the female who was with him now, bringing himself back to the present as he unzipped the leg of Cameo's pants and eased the material up. He grimaced as he saw her ankle was swollen now.

"That's not a good look." She peered at her leg. "Oh my God. It's twice the size of my other leg!"

"It'll be fine. Just needs to be elevated." He gripped her shoulders and eased her onto her back, froze as he found himself leaning over her and her eyes locked with his. The urge to kiss her hit him again, and this time it was harder to deny it.

Because she looked as if she wanted to kiss him too.

He sucked down a breath and forced his eyes away from her, did his best to be a gentleman and not the sort of wild, uncivilised man she probably thought he was because he lived in the middle of nowhere in a basic cabin, with only other men like him in the vicinity. He grabbed the cushions from the worn grey armchair that stood at a ninety-degree angle to the couch near the wall and placed them under her left leg, elevating it until it was above her head. He was probably being harsh on himself, and on her. Maybe it was fear talking—fear that she would take one look at his home, with no running water and only solar power, and think he was a male who wasn't worth anything.

He wasn't sure when he had started wanting her to think he was worth something. He amended that thought. It wasn't being worth something that mattered to him. It was being worthy of something, and he was treading a dangerous path, heading for heartbreak again if he thought she was going to view him as worthy of her heart.

She was human. Nothing could happen between them. Relationships with humans never worked out. Humans were fragile, their lifespan a mere blip compared with his, and they aged fast because of it. He didn't age quickly at all. He was going to look this way, or close to it, for another few hundred years at least. In a matter of years, she would know something was different about him and then what?

He knew the answer to that question.

She would leave. She would realise he was different to her and she would leave, and she would probably take his heart with her and he would spend the next few hundred years feeling like a hollow shell of a male.

Even if he somehow kept his true nature hidden from her, he would have to leave Black Ridge. He would have to leave his brother behind. He would have to leave his pride. He would be a bear alone in a human world.

Just the thought of that made him restless, agitated the more animal part of him, and had him wanting to see his brother, needing to see him and know that they wouldn't be parted.

"Lowe?" Cameo whispered, her soft voice black magic, trying to tempt him to her side. "Is something wrong?"

He shook his head and swallowed hard, avoided her gaze as he checked her ankle. "Nothing. Just tired."

He stood, a little too sharply judging by how Cameo tensed. He issued her an apologetic look and then went to the dresser at the far end of the room, below the window. He opened the cupboard, grabbed the med kit he kept there, and pulled himself together as he checked it had everything he needed. He was being foolish. Hoping for something impossible. As soon as Cameo was able to move, he needed to get her out of his life.

His bear side suddenly growled and snarled, clawed at the cage of his human form. He braced himself against the dresser, gripping the wooden top so hard he feared he would snap it in two as he fought with his other side. That part of him was often grouchy, but he couldn't remember the last time it had been this mad. Fur rippled over his hands and he glared at them, breathed deep and fought the change, unsure why it was coming over him.

It hit him like a thunderbolt.

Both sides of him didn't want Cameo to leave.

Just the thought of never seeing her again was enough to rouse a feral need to roar and lash out at anything that stood between them, filled him with an urge to stake a claim on her, to keep her here in his cabin forever and never let her go.

Lowe stared at the top of the dresser as he let that sink in, as a strange feeling swept through him, one that had him secretly scenting the air, savouring the soft fragrance of Cameo that laced it.

He needed to talk to Knox.

He turned to storm out the door and find his brother, but his gaze caught on Cameo and the need to stay with her easily overpowered the need to speak with Knox. She stared at him, her blue eyes soft and laced with concern, worry not for herself but for him.

Lowe grabbed the med kit and pinned his gaze on the floor, resisted looking at her as he crossed the room to her and set the bag down beside her feet. "I'll bandage it properly this time and then you should probably get some rest. You can take my bed."

He unravelled the makeshift bandage and stared at the dark bruise on her leg.

"In the morning, if the weather is still clear, we can probably call in an air ambulance." He slid a glance at her and she didn't look at him.

She just stared at her leg, a distant look in her eyes, one that made him want to ask what she was thinking. A bubble of suspicion rose up and popped in his mind. She didn't want to leave, and he had the feeling it wasn't because he was amazing company and she just couldn't bring herself to part from him.

Any normal female would want an air ambulance to pick her up and take her away from a group of men in the wilderness. Wouldn't they?

He tore open a pack of crepe bandages and carefully wrapped her leg, glancing at her from time to time, noticing the worry blooming in her eyes. Something was wrong, something that was keeping her silent and putting a war in her eyes.

He pinned the end of the bandage and sat back, stared at her until she finally looked at him. "What is it, Cameo? What are you not telling me? You can tell me."

She swallowed hard, her fine eyebrows furrowing as she looked from him to her leg and then back again. She drew down a deep breath, looked as if she might say something, and then sucked down another.

Lowe sensed the rising tension inside her and the fear, and placed his hand on her knee. "You can tell me. I know you're in trouble, Cameo. I just don't know how deep that trouble runs. I can't protect you from something I don't know about."

A light entered her blue eyes, a flare of hope that quickly died, and she looked away from him and sighed.

"The man that I—" She swallowed hard. "He isn't the only one up here in the valley. There's another. I got him with the bear spray, but what if he was the one who shot the bear? Maybe he wandered into the settlement looking for me?"

That thought clearly shook her.

Lowe was more shaken by her attachment to her bear spray, and the fact his lie about how Saint was responsible for what had happened to the bear she had seen apparently hadn't been convincing enough for her.

"The man didn't shoot that bear, Cameo." He drove that home, all softness leaving his voice now. He needed her to believe the bear had run off and Saint had been the one to do it, giving his alpha a reasonable excuse for his injuries. "But if there's another man up here in the valley, I'll find him... and I'll deal with him. I won't let him near you... but I need to know why they're after you."

Her face crumpled and she shook her head.

Lowe shifted his hand to hers where they rested on her stomach, shuffled closer to her on his knees and stared deep into her eyes. "I need to know, Cameo."

Her brow furrowed again and she leaned her head back, stared at the ceiling for so long he was sure she was ignoring him and wasn't going to answer.

But then her throat worked on another hard swallow and her left hand slipped from beneath his. She unzipped the pocket of her black weatherproof trousers and fished out a phone, unlocked the screen and held it out to him.

"Messages. One from my brother. Nate." She squeezed her eyes shut.

Lowe found the messages and scrolled through them, didn't miss the fact she had sent a heart to her father's number while he had been occupied with Saint or that a lot of unknown numbers had contacted her in the last few months. He clicked on a few of them, cursing himself for snooping, but his gut said the message from her brother wasn't the only disturbing one on her phone.

All of the messages were threats. Demands for money. Threats about killing her parents. Threats about how close they were to finding her.

He bit back a growl as his mood took a dark turn, as a need to head out into the darkness and find the other human in the valley blasted through him. When he found the bastard, he was going to rip him to pieces.

Lowe found the message from her brother and opened it.

Froze.

His blood caught fire, boiled in his veins as he stared at the photo.

He clenched his free hand and set his jaw, stared at the image of someone he presumed was her brother, but the male had been beaten so badly that it was hard to make out his face through all the blood, swelling and cuts.

Lowe went to set the phone down, but Cameo reached for it, hurt and fear in her eyes. He handed it to her and she clutched it to her chest, holding it in both hands, as if it was precious. It probably was. It looked like it was her lifeline—her only way of knowing her parents were safe. He guessed the heart messages they were exchanging were a way of communicating with each other that they were fine.

Still alive.

Unlike her brother.

"Who did that?" He growled those words, on the warpath now, determined to uncover how many people were after her and track every single one of them down.

They would regret coming after her.

They would regret hunting her parents too.

"A man named Karl. I knew him back east. We both did. He got my brother involved in drugs... not taking them." Her voice hitched and she pulled down an unsteady breath. "Nate was dealing them... or handing them out to dealers... or whatever it is people do in that damned business. I didn't know about it until he moved to Vancouver. I thought he was on the straight and narrow. I should've known better."

She looked down at her phone and sighed, a wealth of hurt in it as tears lined her lashes and one slipped down her temple, cutting into her hair.

"They wanted me to help them get drugs over the border and I refused." She sucked down another shuddering breath and exhaled hard, her voice tight as she said, "Nate did something foolish. Apparently, being a drug dealer or whatever he was hadn't been lucrative enough for him... or he made an honest mistake. He... money went missing."

The money the males were now demanding from her.

Lowe frowned at her phone. "Nate got caught with his hand in the cookie jar and figured he could get out of being killed by saying you had the cash."

She nodded. "I don't know what he was thinking."

Lowe did. The male had probably been thinking Karl would let him go and would either target her instead, or make Nate take him to her, and he would have a chance to escape and get the money and flee.

Instead, he had gotten himself killed and painted a target on his sister's back.

He placed his left hand over hers and held them, looked at her fingers as they trembled beneath his as she fought tears.

"I won't let them near you, Cameo," he growled, those words a vow he intended to keep. "What they did to your brother... it won't happen to you. I swear it. You're safe with me."

She looked at him. "I know, but I'm scared. He's out there."

He gently squeezed her hand. "He doesn't know you're here, and if he comes knocking, he'll have more than just me to deal with. I'll warn my brother."

Knox was going to be angry with him when he learned about Cameo's trouble, but his brother would do the right thing.

"You look like you could use some real food, and maybe a shot of whiskey." He reluctantly released her hand and stood, lingered a moment as he gazed down at her and she looked up into his eyes, her blue ones holding a hint of gratitude, and hope.

"I think I just want to sleep," she murmured.

Lowe stooped and lifted her into his arms, gently cradled her to his chest and carried her upstairs to the bed. He set her down on it and she lay back, resting her head on the pillows. He lit the oil lamp on the bedside table for her, kept it low so it didn't keep her awake, and lingered again.

"I'll be just downstairs. Going to fix you some soup in case it turns out you're hungry after all and grab myself that shot of whiskey." He smiled at her and she nodded, the barest dip of her head, and the sight of her hurting had him wanting to stay, needing to be near her and aching with a need to reach down and brush her hair from her face. "It'll be okay, Cameo."

She nodded again and when he went to leave, she grabbed his hand and looked awkward as she held it. "Would you—never mind. Just... thanks."

He knew what she was thinking, what she was feeling. She wasn't a burden, and wanting him to stay close while she fell asleep didn't make her weak. He eased onto his backside on the bed, twisted at the waist and reached over her. He grabbed the blanket and pulled it over her, covering her as best he could.

Her eyes slipped shut and he watched her, monitoring her with his senses, making sure she was calm. How long had it been since she had felt safe enough to sleep without fear? He did growl when he thought about the fact she was running for her life, had been forced to fight a man in order to survive, and there were more still after her and her family. It came out low and deep, a long rumbling sound that he felt sure would make her open her eyes, but they remained closed.

Her breathing levelled out and fell into a slow and steady rhythm, telling him that she was sleeping.

Lowe took the phone from her, switched it off, and set it on the bedside table. He stared at it. Whoever had done that to her brother would pay for it. He would see to that. He would make sure she was safe and free, able to go about her life again.

He lifted his left hand and brushed his fingers across her cheek, lingered with the tips of them against her soft skin, and cursed himself. He was getting in deep again, over his head, and this time he knew things wouldn't end well for him.

He couldn't fall for her.

No matter how badly he wanted to, and no matter how badly he wanted this thing between them to work out.

He had to do the right thing.

He had to let her go.

CHAPTER 9

The smell of frying bacon drew Cameo up from a deep sleep. She yawned and stretched, grimaced as her leg hurt and the wound on her left arm throbbed a little. She sank into the soft mattress, rested her hands on her stomach on top of the fur that covered her and stared at the pitched wooden ceiling as she listened to Lowe moving around below her.

He was humming a tune.

She wasn't sure what it was, but it was strangely comforting, warming even, to hear him going about his life as if everything was normal. Last night, she had felt sure that he would want her as far away from him as he could get her, that she would wake with an air ambulance waiting to cart her away from him. It had surprised her when he had reiterated his vow to protect her and hadn't seemed at all worried that there were men after her—powerful men. Men with guns.

She supposed that living up in a remote valley had probably hardened him in ways she couldn't understand, stripping away his softness, just as it had with his body.

Cameo squeezed her eyes shut and told herself not to think about his body.

A woman could go a long time without seeing such a body in the flesh though, could reach a point where she started believing that men like that didn't really exist, that they were purely in magazines and other more adult things.

"You're up!" Lowe's deep voice rocked her, had her gasping as it shattered a fantasy building in her head, replacing imaginary Lowe with the real thing.

She snapped her eyes open and looked at him, knew how startled she had to look when he rubbed the back of his neck and glanced down the stairs behind him.

"Didn't mean to scare you." He scratched his lightly stubbled jaw. "Just wanted to see if you were in the mood for breakfast? You must be starving."

She nodded, her fantasy of Lowe becoming a fantasy of him draped in that crispy, tempting bacon she could smell. She wanted to eat it off him. That thought startled her more than he had, had her cheeks flaming and her eyes darting to the dark covers and furs on his bed.

His bed.

She grew painfully aware of him as he stood there staring at her, waiting for an answer she couldn't give him while her mind was racing, throwing wicked images at her that she was in no position to be entertaining, and that she certainly would never actually attempt to do.

Her stomach squirmed a little. He was being the perfect gentleman, was taking care of her and making sure she felt comfortable at all times, wasn't being forward with her or making advances, and here she was mentally undressing him and picturing him in compromising positions with her.

Cameo risked a glance at him. Her gaze collided and locked with his, and the banked heat in his blue eyes said that maybe she wasn't the only one indulging in fantasies this morning. She shivered as he stared at her, that heat in his eyes building into an inferno that scorched her, had her aching all over and wanting to reach for him.

She wanted to make him come to her and kiss her. Just a kiss. She swore she would stop at that, wasn't in any condition to be wanting anything else from him. A lie. If he offered her more than a kiss, if he wanted more, then she wouldn't be able to stop herself.

Cameo rolled her eyes closed and fought to master her own body. This wasn't like her. She gripped the front of her cream sweater and pulled it away from her chest, needing some air. Maybe her injured leg had given her a fever and she was delirious.

Maybe she was just attracted to Lowe.

Who wouldn't be?

The man looked like a blond Henry Cavill.

"You feeling all right?" Lowe stepped closer to her and she pulled down a steadying breath, opened her eyes and looked up at him.

"Just a little warm, and I think I slept too long." She grimaced as she sat up, and thanked him with a smile as he rushed to help her, gently took hold of her arm and eased her upright.

He chuckled, the warm sound rolling over her, sending tingles racing through her as it drew her gaze to his face. Blond Henry Cavill. He was gorgeous, especially when he smiled as he was now, forming those little dimples in his cheeks.

Lowe pressed his palm to her forehead and she almost groaned as she felt the coolness of it. "You are a bit warm. You know I had to have the door open half the night to cool down the cabin. You probably just got a little overheated up here. I'll get you some water, coffee and food and you'll feel better."

He didn't sound as if he really believed that. He sounded worried again, which made her worry too. What if her leg was infected?

He dropped his hand to her cheek and stared into her eyes. "You're fine, Cameo. If you're worried, we should call the air ambulance."

She quickly shook her head, the thought of leaving sending a jolt of fear through her. She felt safe here, with Lowe. As much as she didn't want to get him into trouble, pulling him into her problem, she didn't want to leave him. She looked straight ahead of her at the window that revealed part of the cabin that stood in the middle of the clearing and the world around it. A peaceful world. An uncomplicated world. She liked it here.

Lowe sighed. "At least let me get someone to take a look at it, although I'm not sure that she'll help. Maybe the Hippocratic Oath will make her help. Doctors still swear by that, right?"

"There's a doctor up here?" Her eyes widened.

Lowe scratched behind his ear and grimaced. "Not here. She lives just south of here with her ma... man. Husband."

Why had he stumbled over the word man? Had he intended to say something else? She wracked her brain, trying to think of other words that started with *ma*.

Lowe distracted her by sitting beside her and touching her knee. "I can ask her."

She looked into his eyes and caught the nerves in them. For some reason, he was worried about asking this doctor for assistance, and some foolish part of her leaped on that, said that he had fallen out with the husband over her. She shoved that thought aside. Lowe didn't strike her as the sort to go after another man's wife. The attraction she felt to him was making her look for reasons they couldn't be together, had her hunting for flaws that weren't there, and she wasn't sure why. Was she trying to stop herself from wanting him?

It was the most reasonable explanation for her behaviour. She didn't want him pulled any deeper into her mess and getting involved with him would drag him as deep as he could get. It was better that they remained as they were—friends of a sort. Not lovers.

"You don't have to." She eased the blanket off her legs. It cooled them a little, but she was still too warm. Removing her salopettes would go a long way towards fixing that, but the thought of stripping her legs bare in front of Lowe unsettled her, had that heat flaring hotter again. When he looked as if he might touch her overheating cheeks, she rushed out, "I'm being a burden, and I really don't want that."

He pushed to his feet. "It's really no bother."

"It is... I am." She looked out of the window again, at the peaceful world out there, one she felt sure she was close to ruining. "How long have you lived up here? I can't imagine what it must be like to live up here in winter."

Lowe glanced at the window and pulled a face. "A while. Saint owns the land. We all pitch in to take care of things, whether that's repairing the cabins or hunting, or hitting the nearest town for supplies. I know it's not the most modern of places, and I wouldn't say no to running water and power, but I love it here. Everyone up here just wants a quiet life."

"A quiet life," she murmured.

A life she was in danger of ruining.

"Hey now." Lowe eased to a crouch beside her and looked up into her eyes. "You're awfully down this morning. You definitely need a pick me up. Fresh coffee and bacon sandwiches sound good?"

She nodded, but couldn't stop her mood from spiralling downwards. She didn't want to wreck this slice of heaven that Lowe and the others had made for themselves, didn't want to pull them into danger, and she was going to do just that if she remained here.

Lowe's voice gained a hard edge as he placed his hand over hers, curled his fingers around and held it. "Don't think for a second that you're endangering us or that you're better off leaving… sneaking off or doing something crazy. I can handle this trouble for you. *We* can handle it. After all, we're used to dealing with trouble. You should meet our neighbours."

"There are others up here?" She frowned at him.

He had mentioned a doctor to the south, but she had thought perhaps he had been talking about the nearest town.

Lowe nodded. "Whole pack of people a little south of here, closer to the trailhead. Pains in my ass."

He didn't seem to like his neighbours.

He squeezed her hand again. "I'll get you breakfast, and then I'll see about asking the doc to look at you."

When he went to stand and she didn't release his hand, he turned and looked down at her.

"I'd like to come down too." She shifted her gaze to the staircase. Her leg was feeling slightly better this morning, but tackling the staircase yesterday had been close to terrifying and she didn't want to do it again.

Plus, Lowe was right. It was better she rely on him for some things, and asking for his help didn't make her weak or a burden. He wanted to help her.

He smiled and twisted towards her, scooped her up into his arms as if she really did weigh nothing more than a feather. She looped her arms around his neck and settled her head on his chest, relaxed against him as he carried her downstairs, carefully navigating each turn. When he made the final turn, he froze. Cameo looked up at him, wondering what the problem was, and then looked in the direction of his gaze.

She tensed too.

A man stood near the open door, dressed head to toe in black weatherproof gear, his crystal blue eyes stormy as he stared at Lowe and then her.

"Isn't this romantic?" he drawled and unzipped his coat.

Cameo could only stare at him as heat climbed her cheeks and she grew painfully aware of how she was pressed against Lowe, tucked close to his chest.

When Lowe had told her that Knox was his twin, and that they were identical, she hadn't quite believed they would look exactly like each other.

But they did.

The only difference between Lowe and Knox was the colour of their hair, with Knox's a shade darker than Lowe's golden blond.

And the darkness in Knox's gaze.

He slid Lowe a look.

"Yeah, I was about to let her hobble down the stairs." Lowe bit those words out, an uncharacteristically hard edge to his voice as he finished carrying her down the steps and strode to the couch. He gently set her down on it and gave her a worried look. "Not too warm?"

Cameo shook her head. She was a little warm, but with the door open she wasn't in any danger of overheating.

"I'll get you breakfast." Lowe gave her a tight smile that disappeared, turning into a glare as he straightened and pivoted towards his brother. "You want something?"

Cameo had the feeling he wasn't asking Knox if he wanted breakfast too.

Knox grunted as he bent to remove his boots. "All the bacon in the world and an Irish coffee."

"You'll get a third of the bacon and a straight coffee. It's too early to be drinking." Lowe glanced back at his brother as Knox strode to the armchair, peeling his coat off as he went. A worried edge entered his eyes. "You get any sleep?"

Knox tossed his coat onto the back of the armchair and sank into it on a long sigh. He shook his head.

"Saint all right?" Lowe turned to face him now, a plain white mug in one hand and a coffee pot in the other.

Knox nodded and yawned, smacked his lips together and sank deeper into the armchair. "Gods, I need some sleep."

His dull blue gaze slid to Cameo.

"You're pretty. He tell you that?"

Lowe glared at his brother. "Watch your mouth."

"So he hasn't told you that?" Knox smiled slowly in his brother's direction.

"Actually, he has." She had wanted to pick him up on it too. She looked at Lowe, wanting to see whether he really thought she was pretty.

He avoided her gaze, went back to pouring coffee into three mugs.

"Figured as much. We're not going to have a problem here, are we, Lowe?" Knox stared hard at his brother's back.

Problem? Was it that Knox didn't want his brother getting involved with her, or that he thought his brother might try something with her when she didn't want it?

Knox ignored the warning look Lowe gave him and his blue gaze slid to meet hers. "Lowe has too much heart, and it's stuck together with sheer will and a lot of tape, and if you break it, so help me gods, you will pay for it."

Cameo shrank back into the couch and frowned at him. "I have no intention of breaking Lowe's heart."

Because she had no intention of surrendering to the attraction she felt.

Knox grunted, "They never do."

"Maybe I should go back upstairs." She pressed her left hand to the arm of the couch and grimaced as the wound that darted across her upper arm pulsed and throbbed as she tried to stand.

Lowe was quick to grip her shoulder and make her stay where she was.

"You sit." Lowe turned a black look on his brother. "You leave."

"No." Knox made himself more comfortable, wriggling lower in the armchair and stretching his long legs out in front of him as he settled his hands on his stomach and laced his fingers together. "As long as she's here, I'm staying put."

Lowe strode over to his brother, grabbed him by the front of his dark fleece shirt, and dragged him onto his feet. She swallowed hard as he pulled his brother to the door and shoved him out of it, closed it behind him and pushed Knox towards the edge of the deck, far away enough that she couldn't hear them.

But she could see them through the window by the log burner.

Whatever they were talking about, it grew heated, had both men looking ready to throw a punch, and then Knox rubbed his dark blond hair, heaved a sigh and his expression lost its hard edge. He shrugged and said something, worry written in every line of his face.

Lowe pulled him into a bear hug.

Released him and came back to the door, opened it and stepped inside with Knox on his heels.

"He'll be civilised now, apparently." Lowe cast Knox another black look, one that held a warning in it.

"I'm one hungry bear this morning." Knox smiled slightly, as if he had made a joke but it was secret, and slumped back into the armchair. He looked at her, his sapphire eyes softer now. "Sorry about that. I can get a little protective of Lowe."

"I get that." She smiled up at Lowe as she took the coffee he offered her and then looked back at Knox. "I was protective of my brother too."

"Lowe filled me in on that. I'm sorry about what happened to him."

She looked at Lowe for an explanation.

Lowe held a plate out to her, the sight of the two bacon sandwiches on it making her mouth water almost as much as he did as he gave her a soft look. "I hope you're not mad. It seemed like a reasonable way to get my brother to behave himself and stop treating you like you're a threat to me."

She took the plate and held back her smile as he slid another look at Knox, silencing him just as he was about to say something.

"I'm not mad. Relieved maybe." She hadn't been looking forward to having to tell his brother the reason she was here.

She looked from Lowe to Knox. They were both as big as each other, both looked capable and as if they could handle themselves and any trouble that might come their way. She felt as if she could rely on these men, could trust them to help her, but at the same time, part of her still didn't want to get them in trouble.

She ate her sandwiches in silence, sipping her coffee between bites, listening to the fire as it crackled and popped. She tried to think of something to say as Lowe sat beside her, but the thought of having to leave weighed her down, stole her voice and had a war erupting inside her. She had to go. As soon as she was able. Lowe said he could take care of things, and she believed him, but that didn't mean she wanted him to fight her battle for her. Just the thought of him having to fight turned her stomach and put her off her food.

Cameo looked across at him, listened as he complained about the snow to his brother and Knox mused whether spring would come early this year. An ache formed in her chest, a tight knot that felt as if it would only grow worse if she left Lowe.

Just minutes ago, she had been determined to resist the attraction that blazed between them. Now, she wasn't sure she was strong enough to fight it. She wasn't sure she could stay here and not surrender to it, and she couldn't bring herself to leave either.

She didn't want to leave Lowe and it wasn't because she felt safe around him.

She had a terrible feeling it was because she was falling for him.

He was handsome, kind and charming, and he took good care of her. He was the sort of man she had always dreamed of having in her life, and one she had never thought would actually exist. But here he was. Deep in her heart, she knew she would be a fool to fall for him with things in her life so uncertain and danger all around her.

But that same heart also said she would be a fool to deny herself something just because it had come along at an inopportune moment.

She would regret it.

Lowe was a once in a lifetime kind of man, checked every box she could think of, every one she had written down once when she had been lonely in Vancouver, mending her broken heart. It honestly felt as if fate had taken that list she had made and created Lowe just for her.

He angled his head towards her, his eyes slightly wider than normal, as if her staring had disturbed him or maybe worried him. A hint of colour touched his cheeks and he dropped his gaze to her plate and cleared his throat.

"You done?" He stood and took her plate before she could answer, set it down on his and carried them to the kitchen.

Knox gave her a hard look. She held his gaze, refusing to be cowed by him, because she intended to keep her promise—she wouldn't break Lowe's heart.

But that didn't mean she wouldn't steal it.

"Knox, we should, uh…" Lowe gave her an awkward look and then shifted his gaze to his brother. He rubbed the back of his neck. "Check on Saint. We should check on Saint."

Cameo had the feeling that what he really wanted to do was talk to his brother about her and whatever he wanted to say, he didn't want to say it in front of her.

Lowe topped her coffee up and set the pot back on the counter. "Stay indoors."

As if she could go anywhere.

The furthest she could probably make it was the deck and even though the storm had cleared, it was well below freezing out there. She had no intention of making herself feel worse by standing on the deck. She was going to stay right here on the couch, sipping coffee and enjoying the fire and trying not to think about Lowe or her growing feelings for him.

Feelings that part of her said were crazy and the rest said felt right.

He was quick to shove his feet into his boots and pull his coat on, and Knox was just as quick to follow his lead and do the same. They were out of the door in under a minute and as Cameo stared at it closing, a feeling stirred inside her.

Lowe was hiding something from her and something deep inside her said it had nothing to do with her or the trouble she was in.

She pushed to her feet with effort and stared out of the kitchen window in time to see Knox glance back at her and then say something to Lowe.

She had the feeling it wasn't just Lowe hiding something from her either.

Everyone here had a secret.

And she was going to find out what it was.

CHAPTER 10

The heat of Cameo's gaze still seared him, the way she had been staring at him stamping her name on his soul, rousing feelings inside him that had startled him when they had come over him. It wasn't just desire and need her eyes on him had stirred—it had been a powerful need to possess her, a dark need to defend her, and a terrible urge to attack Knox.

Lowe had the feeling it wasn't just because she was beautiful and he was attracted to her either.

These feelings felt more like instincts to him, mastered him in a way he didn't like, easily ripping control from him.

He had felt a powerful need to look at her when she had been staring at him, as if her gaze had commanded him, issuing a silent order he hadn't been able to resist, and his bear side had gone crazy.

Absolutely fucking wild.

The hunger to launch at Knox and take him down, to drive him away from Cameo and ensure the male couldn't steal her from him had startled him and he hadn't been able to stop himself from clinging to what his brother had said.

The fact he had called Cameo pretty.

Knox wanted her for himself.

He growled as he slid a look at his brother.

Knox's fair eyebrows rose high on his forehead as he looked at Lowe. "What's got you so tetchy?"

Lowe had the feeling he knew the answer to that question, but he couldn't bring himself to tell Knox about his suspicions. His brother would only think he was reading into things or looking for an excuse to keep Cameo around, or give in to the desire he felt.

When the answer was all of those things and none of them at the same time.

He had the feeling Cameo was his fated mate.

The one female in this world he could have a mate bond with to form the deepest of connections, one that would allow her to live as long as he did.

He needed to be sure though, feared that he *was* reading into things and seeing what he wanted to see because he was attracted to Cameo, fiercely wanted her and was looking for a reason to give in to that desire. There was no better excuse than a potential mate bond. He could easily blame succumbing to desire on the fact he had thought they were true mates, using the excuse that he had wanted to determine whether they really were fated.

"Something's up with you." Knox slid him a hard look this time, one that Lowe didn't like because it felt as if his brother was trying to peel back his layers, was hunting for the truth and Lowe feared he might find it. "I get that she's pretty, Lowe, but she's human, and we all know how that ends."

Lowe bit back the growl that rumbled up his throat, denying it as the desire to lash out at his brother rode him, compelling him to surrender to it because Knox had called her pretty again. His bear side groaned and battered his will, trying to force a shift, and it was a struggle to hold it back, to stop himself from giving in to it and attacking his brother.

"I know." He bit out instead.

Knox looked at him out of the corner of his eye again. "For a moment there, I felt sure you'd deny wanting her or feeling anything for her, or some bullshit like it. I can read the room, Lowe. The two of you were panting like horny newly awakened cubs."

Lowe scowled at him, because when he had hit maturity at a little over a century old and his sexual instincts and desires had awakened, he hadn't been the one panting and horny, wanting to jump anything that moved.

Knox had.

His steps slowed as he stared at Knox, for the first time really feeling as if he was looking at a darker reflection of himself. Same face. Same blue eyes. Same build. If Cameo looked at him with desire in her eyes, would she look at Knox in the same way? If his brother made a move on her, would she succumb to him?

"I don't like that look in your eyes." Knox's lips flattened, the corners of his mouth turning downwards as his eyebrows knitted hard. "You've got aggression rolling off you like crazy and you look ready to kill me... and I've done nothing wrong. You might want to remember that."

Lowe tried to dial it back, but the urge to strike his brother was strong, the need to alter his face so they no longer resembled each other, so Cameo wouldn't be attracted to him, bringing out his claws.

His brother took a slow step backwards, placing more distance between them, the snow crunching beneath his black boots. "This isn't like you, Lowe. She's got you too worked up. Just take a moment to breathe."

"I can't." He pushed those two words out as fear swelled inside him, the thought he might not be strong enough to tamp down and vanquish the urges surging through him making them sound as desperate as he felt. "Knox..."

His brother closed the distance between them as something dawned in his eyes, brightening them a shade, and clutched Lowe's shoulders, gripping them tightly.

"I'm not interested in the female, Lowe. Whatever crazy ideas are flying around that head of yours, they're wrong." Knox palmed his shoulders, his gaze clear and open, honest. "I'm not interested in Cameo. I'm not a threat to her. I'm not a threat to you. You want to get your heart broken, fine. You want me to stay the hell away from her, I'm good with that. Whatever it takes to fix this."

Lowe stared at his brother, desperately trying to make what he had said sink in. His bear side continued to push for freedom and he continued to fight it, unwilling to surrender to the dark needs running rampant inside him. He didn't want to hurt Knox. Knox had said he wasn't interested in Cameo.

What if that didn't change how Cameo felt about Knox?

"Yeah, I know where this is going." Knox shook him hard enough to rattle his brain in his skull. "Did that work?"

Lowe glared at him and bit out, "Did what work?"

"Just trying to shake that thought loose." His brother slowly smiled. "I'd tease you about the fact you know I'm the better looking of the two of us, but I think you'd rip my head off. I don't like seeing you like this, so I'm going to say a few things and I'm going to say them straight, and you're probably not going to like them."

Lowe growled and bared emerging fangs at him. He did want Cameo.

Knox rolled his eyes, as if he had heard that thought. "Number one. I do not, under any circumstances, want that female you have in your cabin. She isn't my type. She looks like the sort of female who has her whole life planned out right down to the white picket fence and number of kids, and all their damned names. That is *not* my style."

Lowe snarled at his brother. He liked that about Cameo. He liked that she was cautious and planned things, didn't leap before she looked.

Hell, he liked that she struck him as the sort who didn't leap before she did full recon of the entire area and charted every possible problem, had five contingencies in place, and was fully prepared for anything.

Knox shuddered. "You look like you're going to drool, so I'm going to move on. Number two. She does not, under any circumstances, want me. She wants you. The way she looks at you, Lowe... a blind man could see she wants you. Apparently, you're both attracted to the cautious, let's suck the fun out of life by planning everything type."

"Hey." Lowe frowned at him. "I'm not like that."

His brother scoffed. "Yeah... remind me again who it was I caught writing pages and pages of plans after our parents died?"

"Someone had to step up, Knox. Things at the pride were bad and I knew we had to leave, and we had barely a few dollars to our names. I had to find us a place we could settle that wasn't near another bear territory, or encroaching on wolves or cougars." Lowe stepped back, beyond the reach of Knox as regret shone in his blue eyes. "Our parents were dead. We had to leave. Just walking off into the wilderness wasn't an option. It would've gotten us killed."

Knox squeezed his eyes shut and heaved a sigh, stepped up to him again and pulled him into a tight hug. "I know. I'm sorry. You know me. Always shooting my mouth off, saying shit before I fully think it through. I put a lot of pressure on you back then and I'm sorry. I should've been more mature about it. I should've been more like you. I'm lucky you were there. I know that. I probably would've walked right into the territory of another pride or pack and landed in a heap of trouble if you hadn't been there."

Lowe tried to hold on to his anger but it was impossible as he sensed the regret in his brother, laced with pain.

"Mom and Dad dying... I wasn't equipped to handle that and I made you handle it for both of us... and that was a shitty thing to do." Knox squeezed him tightly.

Lowe sighed, wrapped his arms around him and hugged him. "It was hard on both of us, but we made it through... together. I wouldn't have made it without you, Knox. I can make all the plans in the world, but when things go south, you're the one who steps up and takes care of things."

"You do suck at hunting." Knox's voice warmed and softened, the teasing note in it drawing a smile from Lowe. "Probably would've starved without me."

Things hadn't been that dire, but Lowe hadn't been the best at foraging back then, and he certainly hadn't had enough charm to get free meals from females at bars and diners.

"We good?" Knox pulled back and searched his eyes.

Lowe nodded, but couldn't stop himself from adding, "You even look at her the wrong way and I'm not sure I'll be able to stop myself from fighting you."

"That doesn't sound good, Lowe. That sounds a lot like—" Knox cut off as a noise came from Saint's cabin.

His brother broke into a run for the cabin and had mounted the steps before Lowe could even react. Lowe followed on his heels, took the slippery steps up to the cabin two at a time and reached the open door just as Knox was crouching beside Saint.

A very naked Saint.

At least he had shifted back, but Lowe found it hard to take it as a good sign. His alpha was still out cold on the wooden floorboards, hadn't really moved from where Lowe had put him yesterday. He looked around, seeking what had made the noise, and huffed as he spotted the fallen fire iron that rested near Saint's foot. He must have kicked it in his sleep.

"Grab his legs, would you?" Knox glanced at him.

Lowe nodded and moved to Saint's feet, stepping between him and the log burner. The fire was getting low now. He would take care of it once Saint was in bed, wrapped up warm. He stooped and grabbed him by his ankles, hauling him up as Knox held him under his shoulders. Getting him up the twisting staircase proved difficult, but they managed it without bashing his head against the wooden railings or the wall.

He helped Knox set Saint down on the bed and waited with him while his brother went downstairs. When Knox returned with some bandages, Lowe helped him tend to the worst of Saint's wounds, binding them with the cream material.

"Had he shifted back when you left him?" He cast a look at Knox as he settled Saint back onto the mattress again.

Knox shook his head as he drew the covers over Saint. "No. He must have done it shortly after I left. I grabbed some sleep before I came to see you, but I was too tired to sleep for long and I knew you'd want to know what had happened after you had left... plus, I wanted to meet this female you're holding in your cabin."

"I'm not *holding* Cameo. She's not a prisoner. I offered to call her an air ambulance, but she doesn't want to leave."

"Why not?" His brother's eyebrows pinched hard, a dark edge entering his blue eyes, one that reeked of suspicion.

"Nothing nefarious. Just this trouble she's in. Like I told you, there's another man on the mountain looking for her and I told her I could protect her if she stayed with me. I want to help her." Lowe sighed and looked off to his left, out the small window to the white world. "I think part of her is scared of leaving this place and part of her is scared of staying."

Knox grunted. "Can't really blame her. If what you told me is true, then she's been through a lot."

"You didn't see the photograph. What they did to her brother—" Lowe growled, couldn't bring himself to say any more than that. The thought of Cameo ending up like her brother, the fact she feared that would happen to her, roused a darkness inside him that had his bear side roaring for freedom, urging him to head out into the forest and hunt the male down.

Knox clasped his shoulder through his thick winter coat. "We won't let that happen to her, Lowe. She might be worried about getting us involved, but we'll stick to our guns. Whatever shit she's in, it ends here."

Lowe turned and dragged his brother into a tight hug. "Thanks."

Knox patted his back and then twisted away from him, jerked his chin towards Saint. "We should probably let him rest. I'll get washed up and changed, and then I'll come back and check on him."

"I'll get the fire going again." Lowe glanced at Saint one last time to check on him and then headed back downstairs, crossed the room to the log burner and busied himself with building the fire up.

His brother's weary sigh filled the silence as he came down the stairs, as he moved to the deck and out into the crisp morning. Lowe glanced at him. He could feel how worried Knox was and he knew it wasn't only about Saint. Knox was worried about him too, but he didn't need to be. This thing with Cameo wasn't going to end the way his brother thought it would.

At least he hoped it wouldn't.

He closed the door of the log burner, stood and walked to the door of the cabin and out onto the deck. Knox paced back and forth on the compacted snow in front of the steps, the worry Lowe could feel in him only increasing.

His brother stopped just below him, ran a hand over his brow and then tugged his black woollen hat down again. His blue eyes held a flicker of concern as he looked back at the cabin, up at the loft bedroom.

"What's wrong with him?"

"I don't know." Lowe shoved fingers through his ash-blond hair and walked to the steps. He sighed. "It's like he's just given up or something. He shifted back last night and I want to take that as a good sign, but..."

Knox suddenly pivoted on his heel to face the woods.

Lowe had sensed it too.

Scented cougar.

His mood took a dark turn as the female Saint had taken from the Creek stepped out of the woods, her purple woollen hat and scarf brightened by the sunlight. Rather than turning tail and scurrying back to the Creek, she strode forwards, attempting to look brave as she tipped her chin up. It might have worked, but Lowe could scent that she was afraid.

He couldn't blame her for being nervous. Knox was throwing off aggression so fiercely that she had to be able to feel it despite the hundred feet or so of space between her and his brother.

Lowe dropped from the deck to join Knox as he strode towards her, placing more distance between him and the cabin.

"What the hell do you want?" Knox growled, the aggression that rolled off him seeming to spark the same feeling in the cougar female.

Her grey-green eyes flashed with defiance as she straightened even more, standing taller as she approached them.

"I think I left my coat." She was treading on dangerous ground sounding so light and sarcastic while Saint was laid up recovering from serious injuries and what Lowe was beginning to suspect was a broken heart. When she glanced at the cabin beyond them though, her bravado faltered and a hint of fear emerged in her eyes. Her voice lowered, losing its bite as she wrapped her arms around herself, her fingers gripping her green woollen sweater. "I came to see Saint."

"Come to finish him off?" Knox moved into the path of her gaze.

She growled at him, baring short fangs.

"No," she bit out, anger turning her eyes cougar gold. She wanted to fight his brother. It would be a mistake. Knox wouldn't pull his punches this time. That spark of fire was quick to die again, leaving her voice sounding hollow as she said, "I just need to know if he's all right."

Lowe scowled at her, crossed his arms over his chest and came to stand beside Knox, forming a wall with his brother.

She growled again as she took a step forwards, clearly intending to go around them. Both he and Knox moved as one, countering her, stopping her from getting any closer to their alpha.

She ignored Knox and looked at Lowe. Why? Did she think he was the easier of the two of them to convince? Or was it because he had been the only one who had wanted to speak out when Saint had dragged her into the Ridge?

He hadn't agreed with what Saint had done, but that didn't mean he was going to let her get near his alpha again. Saint was hurting and she was responsible for his pain—both the physical and emotional.

She stood in silence, staring at him, a battle raging in her eyes. She wanted to attack him and Knox to reach Saint. He admired her courage and the depth of her desire to see Saint, but starting a fight wasn't going to convince either him or Knox to allow her near their alpha. He stared her down, waiting to see what she would do, part of him willing her to make the right choice and back down.

If she backed down, if she shrugged off her pride and showed him that she was sorry about what had happened, asked him nicely if she could see Saint and assured him that she wasn't out to hurt him, then maybe he would convince Knox to let her past.

"Please. I just want to know he's okay." Her voice was barely a whisper, held a desperate note that made him feel she honestly cared about Saint, that she needed to know he was going to be all right.

He stared into her grey-green eyes, seeking the truth there, trying to see if she did feel something for Saint.

His heart said that she did.

He thought about what to tell her, worry rolling through him as he thought about Saint's condition, together with a spark of hope that she might be able to bring the big bear back to them.

He opened his mouth to speak.

Knox beat him to it. "The state of our alpha is none of your concern, cougar."

She looked between Lowe and Knox, her expression growing defeated, and he could almost read her thoughts. She believed she wouldn't be able to convince them to talk about Saint with her, and she looked close to giving up. Lowe willed her not to. Knox was stubborn, but if she was honest with him, if she spoke the truth and told him the reason she needed to see Saint, then his brother would back down.

"I know you're just trying to protect him," she whispered. "I just need to see him. If you won't let me see him, then at least tell me he's all right. I heard you. You said there's something wrong with him."

Lowe softened towards her a little more. A glance at Knox told him his brother was nowhere near being convinced though.

She sighed.

"I swear, I don't want to hurt him." She looked them both in the eye and Lowe could see in hers that she was hurting, that she was afraid and it wasn't because she was facing him and Knox. She was afraid for Saint. "I don't think I could hurt him."

"Bullshit," Knox snarled.

Lowe grabbed his arm when he went to step forwards and Knox levelled a glare on him, fire blazing in his blue eyes.

"Give her a chance." Lowe looked at his brother. "We're not getting through to Saint, but she might."

Her brow furrowed and she took a step towards them. "What's wrong with him?"

Knox gruffly shoved his hands into the pockets of his heavy black winter coat. "His wounds are healing but he refuses to wake."

"Maybe it's just the winter—"

Knox cut her off. "This isn't that. This is something else. Lowe thinks he's given up."

"Given up?" She looked at Lowe, paling now.

Lowe nodded and looked behind him at the cabin and then back at her. "I found him in the snow. I think he was there for hours. It was getting late by the time I came across him. I got him inside and patched him up. He shifted back and I thought maybe he would wake, but he won't."

The scent of fear rolling off her grew stronger with each word he spoke, a desperate look mounting in her eyes.

She suddenly rushed him and Knox, shoved past them and made a break for the cabin. Knox growled at her and Lowe tightened his grip on his brother's arm, holding him back. When Knox looked at him, he shook his head.

Turned and watched her running into the cabin.

"Let her see him." Lowe glanced back at his brother. "If anyone can reach Saint and bring him back, it's that female."

Knox glared at him. "You don't think?"

Lowe nodded.

"She's his fated one."

He looked at his own cabin, a feeling stirring inside him again, flooding his chest with warmth and rousing a fierce need to return to Cameo.

He surrendered to that need.

Knox gripped his arm this time, stopping him in his tracks, his voice dark.

"We're not done talking."

CHAPTER 11

Cameo hugged the cooling cup of coffee to her chest as she leaned against the kitchen counter, staring out of the picture window, watching Lowe. He had been standing outside the cabin in the centre of the clearing for more than an hour now, talking to Knox, and whatever they were discussing, he didn't look happy.

A little over an hour ago, a woman had appeared from the direction that cabin faced, and Knox and Lowe had spoken with her, had looked as if they were going to run her off their land, but then she had pushed past the brothers and had gone into the cabin.

One of the neighbours that Lowe had talked about?

Cameo's leg ached, a throb echoing along her bones, but she remained where she was, leaned her hip a little harder against the cupboard and kept staring out of the window. She wanted to know what was happening. She wanted to know what Knox was saying to Lowe to make him keep glancing in her direction.

They were talking about her. She knew it. Was Knox trying to convince him to make her leave? She set the coffee mug down and rubbed her right arm as she thought about having to leave this place. Would Lowe listen to his brother? She doubted it. Lowe wanted to keep her here, and she was beginning to feel it wasn't just because he wanted to help her. This attraction she felt wasn't one-sided. Lowe liked her too.

Cameo looked around her at the cabin.

This hadn't been part of the plan.

While she could probably continue her job as a ranger if she lived in a place this remote, it would be difficult. She would have to spend her working days living somewhere closer to where she needed to be, which would only leave the days she wasn't working for her to live here. Would that be enough to make a relationship with Lowe work?

She cursed.

She was getting way ahead of herself as always, planning things ten steps ahead, filling a mental binder with every little detail of how her life would work if she lived with Lowe.

She wasn't even sure that he wanted more than a fling.

She wasn't even sure she wanted more than that.

Her heart called her a liar. She did want something serious with Lowe. She was just scared of it happening.

Her last serious relationship had been with Karl and that hadn't exactly ended well for her.

What if she fell in love with Lowe and he broke her heart?

What if it turned out he was as controlling as Karl had been and tried to make her quit her job and do whatever he said she should do?

It was enough to have her taking a mental step back from Lowe, put fear in her veins and doubts in her head.

She was rushing things, and it wasn't like her, but something about Lowe made her desperate. A little wild. A lot reckless. It was like he brought out a side of her that she had never realised existed. A side that was possessive and also protective, urged her to seize him in both hands and not let him go.

That possessive and protective streak roared to the fore as four men and a woman strode into view from the direction of the woods and Lowe and Knox turned to face them. Both brothers took a few steps towards them and held their hands up, a clear indication to the newcomers to stop where they were.

Who were they?

More neighbours from the south?

She didn't like the way the men gestured at each other, their motions screaming of aggression. The woman she had seen speaking to Lowe and Knox appeared on the deck of the cabin.

A man with blond hair stepped up beside one who had hair a shade lighter, closer to the colour of Lowe's, and stared Knox down.

They were going to fight.

Cameo couldn't stop herself from hobbling to the door and opening it, her heart racing as she thought about the men coming to blows, thought about Knox and Lowe involved in a brawl against four men. She wasn't sure what she intended to do, but she had to do something.

She stepped out onto the deck and limped forwards.

The second she clutched the post that supported the overhanging roof, Lowe looked across at her.

"Cameo, go back inside," he hollered and then turned on the men and said something she didn't hear.

Cameo looked to her right, at the ash-blond man who was staring in her direction too now. Lowe had been speaking to him. The man looked as if he was on the verge of throwing the first punch, which had Knox closing ranks with his brother and saying something to him.

Lowe flicked her another worried look.

Cameo forced herself to take the hint and go back inside, even when what she really wanted to do was storm over to the men and make them leave. She glanced back at Lowe as she reached the door and her heart shot into her throat as he peeled his black coat off and discarded it. The urge to make him stop flooded her, had her pivoting back to face him.

Things looked as if they were going to come to a head when the woman on the deck of Saint's cabin hurried down the steps and pushed past Lowe and Knox, coming to stand in front of them. She argued with the four men, looked for all the world as if she was going to be the one to fight them.

If she did, she wouldn't be alone.

Lowe stepped up beside her and said something to the men, but it didn't defuse the situation. Were they arguing about the woman being on their land, with one of them?

One of the men, the tall one with dark hair, stepped forwards too and spoke to the woman with a gentle look on his face. Her slight shoulders shifted in a sigh and she said something back to him, and then tensed and spun on her heel to face the cabin.

Cameo looked there too.

Her eyes widened as a big man stepped out onto the deck, his presence seeming to defuse the situation, taking everything from a raging boil to barely a simmer as everyone looked at him.

Saint, she presumed.

She grimaced as her leg hurt and bent to rub just above where the ache was worst. Maybe standing on a deck in the cold wasn't the best medicine for her injury, but she hadn't been able to go back inside when Lowe had looked ready to fight. She glanced at him and frowned. Everyone was dispersing now, and the woman was going with the group towards the forest.

Lowe strode towards her, concern etched on his handsome face as he pulled his coat on and his pace picked up the closer he got to her. He swiftly took the steps up onto the deck and cupped her cheek, a tender gesture that flooded her with warmth and made her realise he really did have feelings for her and they were running along the same lines as hers were for him.

His hand was cold as he smoothed it across her cheek, as he angled her head back and looked down into her eyes, his blue ones warm with concern. "You okay?"

She nodded. "Just a little sore."

He cast a worried look at her leg. "You're sure you don't want to—"

"No. I'm fine here." She almost cursed when that came out sounding desperate, scared.

He smiled softly. "Almost sound like you don't want to leave this place."

It wasn't the place she didn't want to leave—it was him. He stared down into her eyes, a sharp edge entering his as they stood in silence, and she had the feeling he was trying to glimpse things she wasn't ready for him to see yet.

She searched for a change in topic, glanced beyond him when the intensity of his gaze began to fluster her, and found it as the big brunet man she believed to be Saint finished buttoning a checked fleece shirt and stepped off his deck.

Heading in her direction.

"What was all that about anyway?" She looked back at Lowe.

He huffed. "Holly lives with our neighbours, but she's taken a shine to Saint, and she came to see him without telling her friends. They were worried about her."

"Is that Saint?" She jerked her chin towards the man marching towards them.

Lowe turned and didn't look happy to see the man closing in on them. He pressed his hand to her waist and eased her back towards the open door.

"You go on inside. Get warmed up." He frowned when she stood her ground.

She wanted to meet the man who owned this place and she had the feeling he wanted to meet her too. Going inside wasn't going to stop this man. She could see it in his dark eyes as he turned a frown on her.

"Knox said we had company." Saint's deep voice rolled over her like thunder, a hard edge to it as he slid Lowe a look that told Cameo he wasn't happy about it.

The second he placed a booted foot on the stairs that led up to the raised deck, Lowe turned on him and pressed a hand to his chest, stopping him. Something passed silently between them as they glared at each other, their faces stern and eyes dark.

Cameo had the feeling she wasn't the only one with a deep protective streak.

Saint gave Lowe a hard look and tried to pass him, but Lowe didn't let him. The man's dark eyes shifted to her and he frowned, narrowing them on her. It didn't go down well with Lowe.

He shoved against the man's broad chest, pushing him backwards so both of his feet were in the snow again.

"We going to have a problem here, Lowe?" Saint slid him a curious look, one that had a sharp edge to it that screamed he didn't like how Lowe was behaving and was close to putting him in his place.

"She's hurt, all right? That's why she's here." Lowe positively growled those words.

It wasn't the truth. Well, it was, but he was omitting something important.

"I'm Cameo. I'm a ranger and… I'm in a little trouble. A lot of trouble. Lowe found me in the woods and helped me." She limped forwards a step so she could see Saint better. "I don't want to be a burden or cause trouble though. If—"

"You're staying," Lowe snarled and flicked her a hard look. "I said I would help you deal with this and I will. We will. Knox will help too."

His blue eyes shifted to Saint.

"I'm keeping my word. Cameo stays here. I'm helping her with her problem and I suggest you don't try to stop me."

Saint looked as surprised as she was as Lowe issued that threat, as he squared up to Saint and glared at him, looking close to punching him.

"Lowe," she said gently and he looked over his shoulder at her, the hard edges of his expression instantly softening. "I don't want you to fight with your friends because of me."

Saint looked from Lowe to Cameo and back again. "Getting awfully territorial for someone who doesn't own this property. I have to remind you who does?"

This was exactly what she had feared. Lowe loved this place. It clearly meant a lot to him. She didn't want him to end up kicked out because of her.

She hopped towards him and placed her hand against his back, on his left shoulder. It was tense beneath her palm, but as he looked at her again, his muscles began to relax.

He huffed.

"Cameo stays." His blue eyes slid to Saint and his voice lost its hard edge. "I need her to stay."

Saint stared at him for a few seconds and then nodded. "We'll talk more about this tomorrow. I was going to suggest you come with me and Knox to the wedding celebration, but maybe it's not such a wise idea. You stay here. Keep an eye on your guest. Make sure she stays inside."

That sounded ominous to Cameo.

She didn't get a chance to ask him what he meant by it though. He walked away from them, heading back towards his cabin, and Lowe was quick to help her inside. His grip on her arm was firm, but she swore his hand was shaking as he helped her to the couch.

Because he had gone from one confrontation to another?

He released her and closed the door, removed his jacket and hung it on the peg. He lingered with his hand on it for a few seconds before turning back to face her. His blue eyes held a worried edge as he ran his fingers through his blond hair, mussing it.

"You shouldn't get into fights with your friends over me." She couldn't hold those words back, needed them out there, needed him to know that she hadn't liked the fact he had almost come to blows with Saint.

He looked over his shoulder in the direction of Saint's cabin and sighed. "I know. It's not like me, Cameo. I swear, I'm not normally like this."

When he looked back at her, his blue eyes were earnest. He closed the gap between them in only two long strides, dropped to his knees beside her and slid his hand along her jaw, turning her face towards him.

"Something about you... Cameo... you make me wild."

A thrill bolted through her, set her blood aflame as his gaze fell to her lips.

Cameo leaned forwards and kissed him, because he made her wild too, made her bold and a little reckless.

He groaned and slipped his hand into her hair, twisted it around his fingers and clutched it tightly as he stole control of the kiss, as his mouth mastered hers and he pulled her closer. She pressed her hands to his chest, trembled at the feel of the hard slabs of his pectorals beneath her palms and how fiercely his heart was beating, matching the frantic pace of hers.

She lost track of time as she kissed him, relishing every sweep of his lips over hers, every tantalising brush of their tongues that stirred heat in her veins, rousing a fierce need for more. She tried to twist towards him to get closer still, aching as fire swept through her, as her mind raced to imagine his hands on her bare skin.

Loosed a muffled grunt as that fire blazed up her leg.

Lowe set her back and looked down at it, and she cursed when she caught the look in his eyes, one that said a kiss was as far as it was going to go. She appreciated that he didn't want to hurt her, but he had to know it was killing her to stop now, when she was just getting fired up.

"I should probably let you rest." He didn't look as if he wanted to do that, not at all.

The heat in his eyes said he wanted to kiss her again, that the God knew how many minutes they had spent kissing each other hadn't been enough for him.

It hadn't been enough for her.

She toyed with the buttons of his shirt, tempted to hook her fingers in the gap between the two sides of it and tug him to her to coax him into kissing her again.

He must have read her mind, because he lifted his hand and curled his fingers around hers, his touch electric, sending a shiver bolting up her arm.

"How about I make us some lunch? I can get some steaks from the larder." He drew her hand away from his shirt and swept his thumb over her fingers. "If you want, I can carry you out there. You could pick what you want from the shelves and the freezer. There's an... ah... outhouse too."

Just the mention of that made her think about how much coffee she'd had this morning and that instantly made her want to use the bathroom, something she had noticed his cabin lacked. It hadn't been a problem before, when she had been slightly dehydrated, but it was a big problem now she had been guzzling coffee and he had put it in her head.

"That does sound good." She glanced at the window above the kitchen sink. "But Saint said I had to stay indoors."

Lowe huffed. "What Saint doesn't know won't kill him. He'll be gone until late. We're the only two here."

It suddenly hit her that they were. She had been kissing Lowe for long enough that they were bound to be alone now thanks to the wedding on the property next door. No Saint. No Knox. Just her and Lowe in a cabin. The wicked glint in Lowe's eyes said he had just thought the same thing.

She held her hand out to Lowe.

When he took it, she pulled him down to her and kissed him again, feeling a little giddy as he claimed her lips, kissed her hard and groaned in a way that sounded a lot like a growl. He swept her up into his arms, pulling a surprised gasp from her lips, and kept kissing her as he turned with her.

Disappointingly towards the door of the cabin and not the stairs to his bedroom.

"Let's go raid the larder." He grinned at her, dimples forming in his cheeks. "I have a recipe I know you'll love."

He was determined to make her eat, but she was determined to keep on kissing him, even if it was the only thing he would do.

"I know what I want for dessert." She stroked the short hair at the nape of his neck and his gaze grew heated as he looked down at her and stepped out onto the deck.

"You do?" Lowe rumbled. "What's that?"

"More of this." She lifted her head and kissed him again.

His grip on her tightened, drawing her closer to him, and he groaned as his tongue tangled with hers.

He broke away from her and breathed against her tingling lips, "Sounds good to me. I want to spend all afternoon and evening kissing you."

She shivered at that, the thought of lazing on the couch just kissing him warming every inch of her. She wanted more, but he was right. She was in no condition to take things further and the sensible part of her was finally making its voice heard, told her that taking things slow was the right way to go.

So kissing him would have to be enough for her.

For now.

But as soon as her leg was feeling better, she would let the wild side he had awakened in her out to play.

She would have all of him.

CHAPTER 12

Lowe was in heaven as he woke with Cameo tucked against his side. He looked down at the top of her head and sifted the fingers of his left hand through her hair, stroking from the dark roots to the blonde tips as he absorbed the feel of her sleeping with her head on his chest, curled close to him. The moment she had settled against him last night, he had wished he had removed his long sleeve white T-shirt so he could feel her skin against his. He wanted to be under the blue covers with her, nude and pressed against her, but when she had gotten sleepy last night, laying with her on top of the covers while she was beneath them seemed like the most sensible thing to do.

He didn't want to rush things.

Which was a change.

With Cameo, he wanted to take his time and savour everything, and he certainly felt as if he had done that yesterday.

A day that had looked as if it was going to turn out bad, had ended up being one of the best days of his life.

Spending the afternoon alone with Cameo in his cabin had been blissful. They had spent most of it making out on his couch, had lazed together and watched some TV shows on his tablet, and then she had fallen asleep in his arms.

Lowe feathered his fingers over her shoulder and angled his head away from her so he could watch her sleeping. She looked so peaceful, as if in his arms was the place she wanted to be most in the world. It was the place he certainly wanted her to be.

Gods, if all he could do was kiss her and hold her like this forever, it would be enough for him.

Someone knocked on the door.

Lowe growled low in his throat, careful not to wake Cameo, the calm he had felt evaporating as he sensed not one but three people on his deck. None of which were Knox. He could feel Saint though.

His alpha had come to talk with Cameo just as he had threatened.

He growled again as he slipped his arm out from beneath her and waited, making sure she was still sound asleep, and then eased from the bed. Saint would just have to wait until she'd had enough rest. She needed her sleep right now. He felt sure her leg was getting better, but she was human and it took time for them to heal. Sleeping would give her the time and rest her body needed to get stronger again.

Lowe padded across the loft floor to the staircase and paused there, looked back at her as she burrowed into the pillows and curled up. An ache throbbed deep in his chest, a need to go to her and shuck his jeans and T-shirt and slide into bed behind her. He wanted to draw her to him and hold her while she slept, her back pressed to his front.

He forced himself to head downstairs instead, rubbing sleep from his eyes as he went.

When he opened the door of his cabin, he wasn't surprised to see Holly tucked close to Saint, her black weatherproof clothing blending with his and her fall of onyx hair spilling from beneath a violet woollen hat.

He was surprised to see the other female who stood just behind the couple—an olive-skinned beauty with rich brown eyes flecked with gold and glossy raven waves tumbling around the shoulders of her oat-coloured jacket.

The doctor from Cougar Creek.

"Saint came to me this morning and mentioned someone was injured." Her voice dropped to a whisper, her dark gaze cautious as she glanced past him into the cabin. "A human. Can I see her?"

Lowe nodded and stepped back, more than happy to let her into his home. "I wanted to come and ask you for help, but I wasn't sure how well it would go down."

He still wasn't sure. One glance at the clearing had him wondering if this was a good idea. Yasmin and Holly weren't the only ones who had come from Cougar Creek to Black Ridge this morning. Flint stood near the firepit with Knox, huddled down into a navy jacket and matching scarf, with his dark woollen hat pulled low on his forehead. The cougar male didn't look happy about being at the Ridge, was scowling in Lowe's direction, and Lowe had the feeling the only thing stopping him from closing the distance between him and his mate was Knox.

"Ignore him. He's grouchy because I insisted on coming. He hasn't got the message yet." Yasmin looked ready to roll her eyes as she glanced at her mate.

"Message?" Lowe frowned at her.

Yasmin looked at Saint and Holly. "We're family now."

He looked at his alpha and could see in his dark eyes as he gazed down at Holly that something had happened between them.

"Congrats?" he said, pleased for Saint and for Holly too.

"Thanks." Saint grinned at him and then down at Holly, tightened his arm around her shoulders and drew her to him for a brief kiss.

It was good to see Saint happy and he was glad things with Holly had worked out.

Some immortals went their entire lifetime without finding their fated one.

He looked up at the ceiling, to Cameo where she slept soundly in his bed, that feeling flowing through him again, one he wanted to draw into focus. Right now, it came and went, and he wasn't sure whether she was his mate or not. If he took the next step with her, he would know without a doubt, but she was in no condition to be intimate with him.

Even when she had given him looks yesterday that had said she wanted to be.

"Follow me. She's resting upstairs." Lowe led the way up to the loft bedroom, Yasmin hot on his heels. He got the feeling she didn't want to linger and upset her mate any more than he already was. Lowe couldn't blame Flint for feeling protective of her. Cougar Creek and Black Ridge had never gotten along, but hopefully the mating of Saint and Holly would go some way towards repairing the rift between the two prides and would be the start of a new day for them, one where they would be friends rather than foes. When he turned a corner in the staircase and noticed the heavy black bag Yasmin was carrying, he held his hand out for it. She waved him away and he shrugged and looked down at Saint, where he stood in the kitchen. "Don't suppose you'd put some coffee on?"

"No problem. I could use some myself. Didn't get much sleep last night." Saint smiled up at him, the smirk of a very happy bear.

Holly slapped his chest and he growled and kissed her again.

Lowe left them to it and carried on up the stairs, crossed the loft to the bed and gently stroked Cameo's hair from her face. "Wake up, Cameo."

She murmured and her nose wrinkled.

"Come on, Cameo. Time to wake up." He tried again.

This time, she frowned and her eyes fluttered open, and she twisted onto her back, a sleepy smile curling her lips.

"I thought you'd wake me with a kiss," she husked, her voice low and laced with sleep.

Gods, he wanted to kiss her. He really did. He stepped aside and her sky-blue eyes widened as she saw Yasmin. She was quick to sit up, a panicked look flitting across her beautiful face.

Lowe glanced at Yasmin and grimaced as he found Saint standing on the step just behind her, a questioning look in his dark eyes. He stared at the male, sure that Saint would say something about what Cameo had said.

Saint just shrugged. "Where do you keep your coffee?"

"Bottom left cupboard." Relief blasted through Lowe as Saint turned away and trudged back down the stairs.

Clearly, staying up all night with his new mate had put his alpha in a very good mood, one where he would even let the fact Lowe had been kissing a human slide.

"I'm sorry I startled you." Yasmin's voice softened, taking on a tone that made her sound every bit the doctor she was. "I'm a doctor from the neighbouring property. I've come to take a look at your... leg... was it?"

Cameo nodded and smiled, her eyes brightening with it as she drew back the blue covers, revealing her bare left leg. Damn, Lowe was thankful that Saint had gone back downstairs because if the male had been up here, he might have erupted in his direction. Just the thought of Saint seeing Cameo like this, so much naked skin on show, was enough to have him wanting to head downstairs to force the male to leave.

"Lowe mentioned there was a doctor nearby." Cameo's gentle voice calmed him, soothing his raging bear side.

In fact, she tamed that part of him so quickly he could only stare at her in shock. His bear side was notoriously grouchy, didn't usually back down when the mood to fight struck him, but something about Cameo had it calm in an instant. Because she was his fated one?

He stared at her, needing to know the answer to that question. He suspected she was, but he could be mistaken. He glanced down at the floorboards as Cameo spoke to Yasmin while she inspected her leg, tuned into Saint and Holly as they murmured things to each other.

Tender things.

Lowe scrubbed a hand over his mouth and looked back at Cameo. He wanted that kind of relationship for himself, wanted Cameo to be the other half of his soul, the one female in this world he could mate with and spend the rest of his life with by binding them together.

Cameo's blue eyes slid to him as Yasmin checked her leg, her look softening as her gaze met his, a warmth emerging in it that drew him to her, filled the darkest corners of his heart with light and worsened the ache in his chest.

She had to be his mate.

He had never felt like this around a female before, both sides of him reacting fiercely to her. Both the bear and the man in him wanted to be close to her, calmed whenever she was near him and raged if she was in danger.

She had to be his fated one.

She smiled slightly, kissable lips curling, tempting him to capture them with his own and spend another day worshipping them.

That smile faltered when Yasmin spoke.

"It's definitely a fracture. Hairline at most... maybe. It's hard to tell without an x-ray." Yasmin offered Cameo a consolatory smile. "It doesn't seem bad though. I would say it should be healed in..." She glanced at Lowe and Lowe gave her a look he hoped conveyed that he knew what she was and what he wanted her to do. She nodded, the barest dip of her chin as she looked back at Cameo. "I'd say no more than two weeks."

Cameo's face brightened. "Really? That soon? That's... wow. That's great. I thought it would be a month or more."

Damn, it was good to see her cheery again. He hated the thought of her being down, let alone actually seeing it and feeling it in her. He wanted her to always smile, even when he knew that wasn't possible. Another mate thing? He would move heaven and earth to make her happy.

"I'll just take another look." Yasmin glanced at him again and then lowered her dark gaze to Cameo's leg as she ran her hands over her shin.

He was going to owe her for this. He knew it and he didn't care. Whatever she demanded of him, he would pay it in order to have Cameo on the mend. There was a reason Yasmin had become a doctor and a reason he had wanted her to take a look at Cameo.

Yasmin had a natural talent for healing others with her touch.

Lowe watched Cameo as Yasmin worked, knew the moment she had given Cameo's healing a boost because Cameo suddenly looked even brighter, the fatigue that had been in the depths of her eyes and the dark shadows beneath them disappearing.

Yasmin leaned over and fumbled around in her bag, pulled out a black brace and held it against Cameo's leg, measuring it. "It should fit."

She opened the straps and set it on the bed, took out a cream support bandage that looked a little like a long fabric tube to Lowe, and eased it on over Cameo's leg.

"Does that hurt?" Yasmin glanced at her as she carefully drew the tube of material up over her shin.

Cameo stared at her leg and shook her head.

"That's good." Yasmin finished with the bandage and set Cameo's leg into the brace. It covered her leg from foot to knee, resembling a plastic padded boot. The last time Lowe had seen a cast, it had been made of white plaster. This new version was ingenious, would mean Cameo could remove it if she needed to. Yasmin tightened the straps and checked it over, making sure it was snug. "How does that feel?"

"It feels great." Cameo's blue eyes shone, dazzling him and making him want to smile.

She glanced at him and a hint of colour touched her cheeks, a spark in her gaze that spoke to him on a deep, primal level. She was thinking wicked things. He swallowed and ran a hand over his mouth again, tried to ignore the way that spark ignited his blood and had him itching to make Yasmin and the others leave so he could be alone with Cameo.

Yasmin rifled through her bag again and held something out to Cameo. "Take them if the pain is too much. Go easy on them though. They're strong."

Cameo took the plastic bottle and stared at it as she nodded.

"You'll still need to be careful with the leg. Don't put too much weight on it and rest it as much as possible." Yasmin's voice took on a harder edge, one that had Cameo nodding and looking at her. The raven-haired female stood and grabbed her bag. "I think I'm done here. I'll come by in a week to check on you. If you need anything, just send Lowe to the Creek."

Cameo kept nodding.

Yasmin looked at him as she turned and walked towards him, and he dipped his head, silently thanking her for helping Cameo.

He waited for her to head downstairs before he went to Cameo, leaned over her and tunnelled his fingers in her hair. He tipped her head back and captured her lips, kept the kiss tender and slow, an outpouring of his feelings for her.

When he eased back, she smiled hazily at him.

"There's your good morning kiss." He smoothed his palm across her cheek.

She sighed. "It was worth waiting for."

His thoughts exactly.

"Lowe. Coffee." The hard edge to Saint's deep voice had Lowe tensing and releasing Cameo.

His alpha wanted to talk and he wanted to talk now.

"I'll grab you a cup." Lowe dropped a kiss on her lips and then pivoted away from her, hurried down the stairs to find Saint alone in his kitchen.

The big brunet bear jerked his chin towards the deck as he thrust a white mug of black coffee at him. Lowe took it and followed him outside, closing the door behind him. Holly and Yasmin were walking back across the clearing, heading for Saint's cabin, and Saint stared after his mate, a heated look in his dark eyes.

"Knox told me a little about your guest and now I'd like to know the rest." Saint didn't take his eyes off Holly.

Lowe sipped his coffee, got his thoughts lined up and told Saint everything, filling him in on all that had happened from the moment he had heard the first gunshot to when Saint had met Cameo.

Saint grunted. "Humans."

He was preaching to the choir. Immortals had their issues with each other, but shifters didn't tend to start wars within their own species and it was rare for them to hunt another in the way the drug dealers were hunting Cameo.

Saint scratched his beard and huffed, his gaze still locked on his mate. "If trouble rolls into Black Ridge, we'll deal with it. Knox managed to get in touch with Maverick and Rune. They left Vancouver straight away and should be here before the day is out."

That was a relief.

He stared at Saint's profile, grateful for the help he was offering to Cameo, something Lowe was deeply aware he didn't need to do. Saint would have had every right to make Lowe take Cameo away from the pride in order to protect them. The big bear had a big heart buried beneath his growly, take-no-shit exterior though.

Lowe had the feeling Holly had stolen it.

That feeling only grew as Saint absently held his empty coffee mug out to Lowe and took a step towards the edge of the deck as Holly strayed further from him. Lowe barely managed to catch the mug as Saint released it, clearly not aware of what he was doing.

Too swept up in his mate to notice that Lowe hadn't taken the damned thing from him.

"Take care of Cameo." Saint slid him a look, a sly edge to his smile, and then he dropped off the deck and hurried towards his mate across the compacted snow.

Lowe looked over his shoulder, up at the loft, hunger to do just that riding him hard. He turned and went back inside, set Saint's empty mug down on the counter and grabbed a fresh one for Cameo. He filled it to the brim and carried it upstairs with him, stopped at the top of them to drink her in as she looked across at him, her blue eyes still bright. She looked so at home in his bed beneath the pitched wooden ceiling of the cabin, as if she belonged there.

Gods, he felt as if she did.

She belonged with him.

"You're looking better already." He held the mug out to her rather than setting it on the wooden nightstand and a shiver tripped through him as she took it, her fingers brushing his.

"I'm feeling better already." That heat was in her eyes again, making him burn for her.

He caught a flicker of worry in them too though.

He pushed aside thoughts of kissing her and sat beside her instead, watching her as she sipped her coffee and that worry began to build.

"If those men come here, we can handle it." He settled his hand on the covers over her knees. "Saint says that Rune and Maverick are on their way back."

"And that's a good thing?" She looked as if she needed to hear that it was.

He nodded and tried to think of the best way to sum up the duo. "They're capable. Strong. They used to be cage fighters."

She brightened a little again at that and part of him wanted to growl at the fact she was thinking that Rune and Maverick would be better at protecting her. He wanted her to only need him, even when he knew he was being ridiculous and possessive, and that it was better if she had all five of them protecting her.

"No one is going to hurt you, Cameo. I won't let them."

Her blue gaze strayed to the window behind him, a distant and troubled edge to it. "When he grabbed me, that man said that Karl was coming. He should be here by now. I don't know whether the other man went back to the road. What if he contacted Karl and gave him this location? He might have seen me here."

"Try not to stress about it. We can handle it." He rubbed her right knee through the blue covers, careful not to disturb her left leg.

A flicker of panic lit her eyes. "You keep saying that, but what if you can't handle it? What if he brings all of his men? What if they're all armed to the teeth? Do you even have guns here? I haven't seen any."

Her voice rose with each word, the tension he could sense in her increasing with every question she threw at him, and he wanted to pick her up on the fact she had searched the cabin for a weapon but let it slide, because calming her took priority.

"Cameo, I'm sure—"

Her eyes were wild as she snapped, "You don't know Karl!"

Lowe frowned at her. "And you do?"

She fell silent, her gaze dropping to her coffee as she clutched it before her, her knuckles turning white from the fierceness of her grip. He scented fear on her and her heartbeat was off the scale. He palmed her knee, trying to get her to look at him, needing her to answer his question because those primal instincts she triggered in him were starting to go as wild as her eyes had been.

If she didn't answer him soon, he was going to head out and hunt the bastard down to get the answer from him instead.

She sighed, set her mug down on the bedside table, and closed her eyes. "Karl is my ex. He wasn't a criminal when we were together, but… there was always something about him. Something dark. It didn't take me long to realise he was a violent man. A driven man."

She opened her eyes and lifted her head to stare deep into his.

"Karl wants his money... money I don't have... and I fear he'll do whatever it takes to get it... even hurt those I care about."

The way she looked at him as she said that, the way her eyes softened to reveal nerves and a hint of affection, had the hunger to hunt Karl down and kill him falling away.

He fell into those eyes instead, warmed to his bones by her veiled confession.

He wasn't the only one falling in love.

He reached his hand out and seized her nape.

Dragged her to him and kissed her.

CHAPTER 13

Cameo's moan was sweet music to his ears as Lowe kissed her, as his tongue stroked the seam of her lips and she opened for him. Her tongue brushed his, sent a thousand hot prickles rolling down his spine and had him on the verge of growling. He came dangerously close to doing just that as she wrapped her arms around his neck and dragged him down with her as she fell backwards onto the mattress.

Lowe groaned instead and pressed his hands to the bed, reluctantly broke the kiss and levered himself up so he could see her face. He needed to look into her eyes and see she knew where this was going. He needed to know she wanted it, even when he could sense it in her. His heart drummed against his chest, a powerful beat he swore she was in control of as she smiled up at him, making it skip.

"You sure about this?" His eyes darted between hers, twin worries arrowing through him.

He feared this would just be an outpouring of need, the scratching of an itch for her when he knew it would be so much more for him. He feared he might accidentally hurt her too. Yasmin had given her healing a push, helping her along, but he was sure her leg had to hurt still.

A third worry emerged as she nodded, her blue gaze sultry and hooded as it fell to his lips, beckoning him to kiss her again.

What if he lost control?

She was human, fragile, and his bear instincts were already roaring to the fore, demanding he take her, that he stamp his mark on her and claim her. He struggled to hold back those needs, stared at her and tried to tame them with the sight of her.

"What is it?" She lifted her right hand and gently brushed her fingers across his forehead, her touch black magic as she drifted to his hair and stroked it.

"I'm afraid I'll hurt you," he croaked, meaning it in two ways, or maybe more. He wasn't just worried about hurting her leg or being too rough with her while he was lost in the throes of passion. He was worried about hurting her emotionally too.

Some humans didn't react well to the knowledge that there were shifters in this world.

And she *would* find out that he wasn't like her.

He couldn't keep it from her forever. If things got serious between them, he would have to tell her. He could probably go years without having to tell her, but at the same time, he couldn't. He couldn't do that to her. He couldn't live a lie with her, keeping an important part of himself secret, hidden from her. If this thing between them turned out the way he wanted it to, then he would tell her as soon as he was sure of her feelings.

And if she walked out on him, he would just have to find a way to deal with that.

"You won't hurt me, Lowe." She dropped her hand to his chest, her palm warming him through his T-shirt. Her gaze was sincere as she looked deep into his eyes. "I'm not in pain right now and if I start hurting, then we'll stop. Okay?"

He nodded.

Her faith in him floored him, had the rest of him warming as he gazed at her and realised it was already too late for him.

He was in love with this courageous, kind and beautiful female.

He focused on that feeling as he dropped his head and kissed her. She responded by grabbing the hem of his T-shirt and pulling it up his back, her eagerness bringing a smile to his lips. He broke the kiss just long enough for her to tug his T-shirt off over his head, seized her lips again as he wrestled his arms out of it and tossed it aside, not caring where it landed.

Lowe pulled the bedclothes aside and pressed his forehead to hers, looked down at her chest and wanted to growl at the sight of her in one of his T-shirts. The grey material hugged her breasts, did nothing to conceal the hard peaks of her nipples. He eased back and settled on his knees between her legs, skimmed his hands up over her thighs, shaking a little as nerves got the better of him.

Cameo moaned and arched, stretched her arms out above her head. He glanced at her, groaned as he caught sight of her with her eyes closed and her breasts jutting up, a look of bliss on her face. He pushed the hem of the T-shirt up, revealing her plain black cotton panties and then the flat plane of her stomach. He leaned forwards, pressed kisses to that expanse of smooth, pale skin as he ventured higher, his gaze fixed on her breasts.

His cock kicked hard as he revealed them, as their dusky rose peaks called to him.

Lowe swooped on the left one, savouring Cameo's gasp and the moan that followed it as he sucked and swirled his tongue around her nipple. She jacked up off the bed, her stomach pressing against his chest and the apex of her thighs rubbing his stomach. He groaned and gripped her backside, keeping her pressed against him as he kissed his way across to her right breast, sucked that nipple too, eliciting another moan from her.

An urge to tear her panties from her ripped through him and he fought it, pulled back on the reins and focused on being gentle with her—making love with her. He wanted that. He wanted this to be about more than a physical connection to her. He wanted it to be an emotional one too, a strengthening of their growing bond.

Cameo had other plans, tried to derail his by reaching for his fly, her fingers swiftly tackling the buttons. He groaned and shuddered, lightly bit her nipple as she slipped her hand into his jeans and palmed his rigid length. His head went a little hazy as she stroked him, as her fingers teased him, each brush of them sending heat rolling through him, cranking the temperature of his blood up another degree.

She groaned in time with him as she wrapped her hand around him.

Gods.

If she was trying to get him to make a fool of himself, she was doing a good job of it.

He caught her hand before she could bring him to climax and eased back, didn't miss her slight scowl as he stole her fun from her. That frown melted away as he dropped from the end of the bed to stand, as he shoved his jeans down and stepped out of them, kicking them aside. Heat blazed in her eyes as she raked them over him, her pupils devouring the aquamarine of her irises as she drank her fill, leaving no part of him untouched by her searing gaze.

He groaned and flexed, his length kicking as his muscles tensing tore another sultry moan from her, had her gaze growing darker and the scent of her need growing stronger. She licked her lips and dropped her hands to her hips, eased her panties down at an agonisingly slow pace. Teasing him now? He hadn't been teasing her when he had flexed. It had been an involuntary reaction to the feel of her eyes on him, an instinct that had hijacked him and made him show her just how strong he was.

Lowe scrubbed a hand over his mouth as she revealed dark curls, as she lifted her knees to skim her panties over them, flashing the peachy globes of her backside.

She huffed.

He shook himself out of his hazy reverie and looked at her face, wanting to know what was wrong. Her lips compressed as she wrestled with her underwear and he realised what the problem was. Her cast had got in the way of her sexy reveal.

She gave up trying to get the left leg of her panties over it and shrugged. Looked at him.

Beckoned him with a crook of her finger.

Lowe growled, managed to make it sound like a groan, and mounted the bed. He caught her right leg and pulled her to him, moaned again as he settled between her thighs, as she lifted her right knee and pressed it to his waist, opening to him.

She threaded her fingers in his hair as she kissed him, breathless moans escaping her as he rubbed between her thighs, gliding along her slick heat.

He groaned and kissed her harder, slipped his right arm beneath her and lowered his left one, skimming it down her side.

"Cameo." He pulled back and gazed down at her, struck by her beauty all over again, by the instincts she stirred in him, ones that were growing stronger and clearer by the second.

He needed her.

The heat in her blue eyes said that she needed him too.

That she wanted him.

Lowe slipped his hand between them, gripped his shaft and eased back. He groaned in time with her as he slipped the blunt head through her folds, as he found her core and eased inside, savouring their first joining. Her eyelids drooped, her gaze growing hooded as he filled her, slowly easing into her.

Her hands gripped his shoulders, fingertips pressing into his muscles, and she moaned, another little breathless one that sounded more like a gasp as she stretched around him.

"Lowe," she whispered, a plea and a demand in his name, and damn, he liked the way she said it, as if she couldn't get enough of him, might go mad without him or if he didn't do what she needed him to do.

He covered her with his body, tangled his left hand in her hair as he rested his weight on his right elbow, and kissed her as he began moving inside her. Each long, slow stroke was torture and bliss rolled into one. He swallowed her moans as he thrust into her, trying to keep the pace of them leisurely, a tender joining of their bodies and entwining of their souls.

He drew back and looked down at her again, lost himself in her eyes as they moved together. The instincts grew stronger, clearer still, and he couldn't stop himself from gripping her nape, from holding her at his mercy as he pumped her, curling his hips to reach all of her. She didn't seem to care that he was holding the back of her neck, keeping her in place.

In fact, she seemed to like it.

She moaned and arched against him, pressed her nails into his shoulders and then shifted her right hand to his nape. Her face screwed up as she gripped it hard, digging her fingertips into it, sending a thrill bolting down his spine that had his cock growing harder still and came dangerously close to wrenching control from him.

He growled and dropped his head, seized her lips and kissed her hard as he began to pump her faster. He shifted his weight to his left elbow and gripped her hip with his right hand, lifted her slightly and relished her sweet cry as he plunged deeper still. Her nails scored his nape, sent heat blasting through him to make his thoughts hazy as he felt the sting of them raking over his skin. Another growl pealed from him as he took her harder, unable to hold himself back as she pushed him deep into his instincts.

His fingers flexed against her nape, his claws emerging as the hunger to bite her there mounted inside him, threatening to tear what little control he managed to retain from him.

He drove into her again.

Groaned and shuddered as she cried into his mouth, as her body trembled and throbbed around his, shattering the urge to bite her as her release triggered his, had seed boiling up his cock. He breathed hard with each hard pulse of his length, heat and tingles racing through him as he gently thrust into her, as he pressed their bodies close together and clung to her.

Sweet gods.

She sagged beneath him, her breath leaving her on a contented sigh that had calm washing through him.

Lowe sank against her, kissed her slowly, softly, savouring the warmth and the deep sense of connection that rolled through him. He felt her smile against his mouth as she stroked his back, as she feathered her fingers down his chest and kissed him, was sure she was feeling the same way as he was, swept up in this moment, deeply aware that what they had was something special.

Once in a lifetime.

Something she confirmed for him as she eased back and her eyes darted to her nails, widening as she stared at them. "Oh my God. I'm sorry. I didn't mean—"

He silenced her with a kiss, one he hoped would chase her worries away, because he wasn't angry that she had clawed his nape so hard she had drawn blood.

He was overjoyed.

Because her reaction to him could only mean one thing.

Cameo was his fated mate.

CHAPTER 14

Cameo nursed her coffee as she stood on the deck of Lowe's cabin, enjoying the afternoon sunshine, not feeling the bite in the air as the warmth of the log burner escaped the open door behind her and heated her back. She stroked her fingers over the soft material of the cream sweater Lowe had taken great pains to clean for her, idly shifting them back and forth. She couldn't stop smiling as she took in Black Ridge, and it wasn't only because the valley was beautiful, with its towering white peaks bright against the clear blue sky and snow-dusted pine forest.

It was because her leg was already feeling better, wasn't causing her any pain. Lowe had given her a pair of too-large black sweatpants that fitted over her cast, and it was nice being in something clean and being more mobile.

It was because she felt incredibly sated. She had never been with someone like Lowe. What they had shared had been intense, incredible, and she wanted an encore, but Lowe had needed to speak with Saint and Knox about something and had left her with only a kiss when she had tried to get that encore going.

Cameo was sure that it was because of what she had told him about Karl.

Just thinking that name was enough to set her on edge, had her casting her gaze over the cabins situated around the clearing and then the trees that surrounded her on all sides. How long would it be before Karl found this place? She hoped the answer to that was never. Karl wasn't the kind of man who enjoyed mountains and the great outdoors. He preferred cities.

The sensible part of her said that wasn't going to stop him from coming after her.

The only way to stop him was to get him his money or deal with him.

Her stomach squirmed at the thought, at how easily she could think about killing him and his men. It wasn't like her, and she knew deep in her heart that even if she had the opportunity to take him down, when it came down to it, she wouldn't be able to go through with it. She wasn't a killer.

Was Lowe?

She hated herself for thinking that. Lowe was kind. Gentle. Didn't strike her as the sort of man who would murder someone. She looked at the mountains again. He did live up in this wild place though and he did seem able to handle himself. If it came down to it, she felt certain that Lowe would do whatever it took in order to stay alive or in order to protect her.

Her thoughts drifted to the mountain, to when the man had grabbed her and how she had reacted. She had fought him. The instinct was there inside her too and she had the feeling that if she saw Lowe in danger or was facing death, she would find the strength and courage to do the unthinkable.

She wasn't sure what that made her.

Cameo looked down at her feet and sipped her coffee, tried to distract herself from her dark thoughts. She wriggled the toes of her left foot, pleased when her leg didn't ache. She had taken one of the pills Yasmin had left for her this morning when her leg had been a bit sore, and they had been quick to steal that pain away. She smiled. Her feet looked so funny with one in a black plastic cast and the other in a boot. It made her lopsided too. The heel of her boot was higher than the one on the brace. Lowe had chuckled about that when he had found her walking around his cabin, testing her leg because she had wanted to get some fresh air.

The need to see Lowe that had been steadily building inside her reached a crescendo and she willed him to come back to her. She wanted him to take her mind off everything and she knew just the way he could do it.

She lifted her head and took another sip of her coffee, and her smile widened as Lowe stepped out onto the deck of Saint's cabin, as if he had felt her need of him, and quickly took the steps down to the compacted snow. He turned towards his cabin, his stride hitching as he spotted her and then falling back into an easy rhythm as he strolled towards her.

Cameo wanted to growl at the sight of him.

He looked more than good with his dark green and black checked fleece hugging his broad chest and navy jeans tightening across his powerful thighs with each step. He looked like a predator on the prowl as he closed the distance between them, and she shivered as she stared into his eyes, aware that when he reached her, he was going to eat her whole.

Lowe suddenly spun away from her, twisting to his right and landing hard in the snow.

The gunshot reached her ears a split-second later.

"Lowe!" Cameo darted for the steps of the deck, shrieked as another bullet tore through the wooden post to her right and fell back towards the cabin door, dropping her mug.

It smashed as it hit the wooden boards near her feet.

Cameo stared at Lowe where he lay in the snow, breathing hard as adrenaline surged through her, making her limbs shake and heart race. Her eyes widened as she tried to figure out what to do, as Saint stepped out onto the deck of his cabin and immediately ducked back inside as a bullet ripped into the side wall of it.

It hit her that there was only one way to save Lowe.

She stared at him as he rolled onto his back, leaving a deep crimson patch on the snow.

She didn't want to leave him, but if she remained, she would end up getting him killed. She glanced at Saint's cabin. She would end up getting them all killed. She couldn't let that happen. She had to do something.

Lowe looked at her, their eyes locking, and in that heartbeat of a moment she knew that he knew what she was going to do.

She smiled for him and then hurried down the steps to the snow and broke left, heading for the trees that lined the edges of the clearing, running north as quickly as she could manage.

"Cameo, no!" he bellowed.

Her heart ached as she forced herself to keep running, ignoring the urge to turn back and go to Lowe. She had to do this. She had to draw the man away from the people who had been so kind to her.

From the man she was coming to love.

Her breath fogged the chilly air as she ran, the cold swift to invade her sweatpants and slip icy fingers through every tiny crevice in her cream sweater. Her leg began to ache, but she pushed onwards, into the trees, and shrieked as a bullet ripped through the trunk of one she had just passed. She ducked and kept running, her heart shooting into her mouth to drum there at a fierce rate as adrenaline surged again.

Threatening to make her legs wobble beneath her.

She held it together and kept running, determined to lead the man away from Black Ridge, unsure what her plan was once she had achieved that. Would Lowe come after her? Every instinct she possessed screamed that he would. He wouldn't let her fight this man alone.

She glanced back over her shoulder as she veered right, following the forest around, heading back towards the centre of the valley.

Bit back another shriek as a deer exploded from the bushes ahead of her, bouncing off into the distance.

The man fired again, the bullet whizzing past her as she ducked and fought to remain upright and keep running. She moved around a dense shrub and ran in a straight line with it at her back, hoping it would make it harder for the man to see where she was going.

The ache in her leg worsened, becoming a throbbing that had a pulse of heat shooting up to her thigh whenever she placed her weight on it. She wasn't sure how much longer she could keep running.

She cursed herself.

She should have come up with a better plan before breaking cover. This wasn't like her.

But the thought of the man killing Lowe had propelled her into action.

She didn't want to die, but this was her problem, not Lowe's. If anyone was going to be caught or killed, it should be her. Not that she intended for either of those things to happen. She rounded a stony cliff and paused, sure she recognised it. The place where she had spent the night with Lowe. Her first instinct was to hide inside, and it was hard to resist the urge as adrenaline and fatigue caught up with her, panic making her head hazy as her thoughts collided. It would be a mistake. The man was bound to check it.

Cameo kept running instead, heading past the small cave, moving north still.

Boulders dotted the land, heavy with moss and snow, surrounded by towering pines that offered her little cover. She moved from rock to rock, trying to use them to conceal her trail, making it hard for the man to spot her. She rounded a large boulder and exited on the other side of it.

Threw herself back behind it when a bullet pinged off the rock, ricocheting into the trees.

She landed hard on the dead brown pine needles and twigs, grunting as the air burst from her lungs and her leg throbbed madly. She clutched it and shuffled back onto her feet, gritted her teeth as the pain grew more intense. She had to keep moving.

Cameo looked around her at the forest.

Cursed when she realised she had run into a shallow bowl, one that had a steep slope surrounding it on all sides except the direction she had entered from. The thought of heading back the way she had come had her pulse pounding faster, so she made a break for the section of slope that looked the easiest to scale.

She scrambled up it, grabbing roots and saplings, her teeth clenched hard as every step she took had pain rolling through her.

Screamed as someone grabbed her left leg and pulled her backwards, slamming her face-first into the dirt. Cameo reacted on instinct, kicked out with her booted right foot and nailed the man in his face. He grunted and lost his grip on her. She scrambled forwards, desperate to reach the top, her heart thundering so fast she feared she would pass out.

The man grabbed her again and yanked her towards him, flipping her onto her back this time, and all thoughts of kicking him fled her mind as she came face to face with the barrel of his rifle.

Cameo swallowed hard and sank against the ground.

It was over.

A vicious roar echoed through the trees.

CHAPTER 15

Fire pulsed in powerful waves across Lowe's right shoulder, stealing his breath as the snow beneath him stole his body heat. He grunted as he tried to move and growled through his fangs as they descended and he made it into an upright position. He shoved his hand to his shoulder, grimacing at the slick warm patch on his fleece shirt, and got his left foot beneath him. Pain ripped across his ribs as he lumbered onto his feet and condensed in his heart as he stared in the direction Cameo had gone.

His bear side roared for her to come back, even when the human part of him knew the reason she had run.

She had done it to protect him.

She didn't want him pulled deeper into her trouble, into danger because of her, but he couldn't let her do this alone. He had told her that he would help her and he meant to keep that promise.

"Lowe, wait!" Saint barked, but Lowe wasn't listening.

He gripped his shoulder and ran, following the trail Cameo had left in the snow.

His heart pounded hard against his ribs as he raced through the trees after her, growls rolling from his lips as he thought about her in danger. Fur swept over his hands and his fangs elongated, but pain stopped his bear side from emerging.

He leaped over a fallen tree and landed hard on the other side of it, broke right as he scented Cameo in that direction, together with the disgusting smell of gun oil. Another snarl rumbled in his chest and fur raced over his hands again. The bastard would pay for shooting him. He would pay for daring to chase after Cameo.

His thoughts darkened as his instincts seized hold of him, roused by Cameo being in danger. His nails transformed into claws and he had a hard time resisting lashing out at everything that got in his way as he thundered through the forest, tracking her scent.

When her scream tore through the trees, it was game over.

His bear side roared to the fore despite the pain he was in, had the change coming over him so swiftly that it made him feel sick. His muscles expanded as his bones shortened in places and lengthened in others, his clothes tearing as his body grew in size. He landed on his front paws and kept running, shaking off the remnants of his clothing and kicking off his boots.

He roared as his paws pounded the dirt, as he scented Cameo's fear. It drove him deep into his instincts. They swallowed him and the pain in his shoulder disappeared as a single need consumed him.

Save Cameo.

Protect his fated mate.

She shrieked again.

Lowe thundered forwards, the hunger filling his mind growing darker as her scent and that of the man grew stronger. He was close. He growled as he caught sight of something through the trees ahead of him, shook his head and flashed his fangs as he realised it was Cameo, desperately trying to make it up an incline.

She fought bravely.

His beautiful mate.

When the man flipped her onto her back and shoved a gun into her face, Lowe lost it.

He ran harder.

Roared as he leaped onto a huge boulder in the middle of the bowl-shaped clearing.

He kicked off it as the man dressed all in black swung towards him, bringing his rifle up, moving it away from Cameo. She stared wide-eyed at

Lowe, her blue eyes filled with fear, terror he knew in part was because of him.

It didn't stop her from reacting though.

She kicked the man in his stomach with both feet, launching him backwards. He lost his grip on the rifle as he hit the dirt on his back. Lowe snarled as he charged him, taking advantage of the fact he was unarmed.

The human reached into his jacket and pulled out a handgun, had squeezed the trigger before Lowe had time to react. The first bullet ripped past him and the man adjusted his aim. Lowe growled and turned, banking left, dodging the next bullet. He kept weaving, his larger form making it hard to avoid being shot as the man unloaded the gun.

He came back around the boulder, growling when he saw he hadn't managed to draw the man away from Cameo at all.

Her wide blue eyes gained a flicker of something as she stared at Lowe.

They darted to the man's back as he reloaded.

And then she was on her feet and leaping onto his back.

The man grunted and tried to shake her, hitting her with his elbow as he twisted and turned. Cameo clung to him, battering the side of his head with her fist whenever she could manage it.

Lowe thundered towards the male, using the opening she had given him.

He reared up onto his hind legs and splayed his front paws, aiming them at the man's head, hoping Cameo had enough sense to make a fast exit. Her eyes locked with his and he could see in them that she knew what to do.

She struck the man one last time and then heaved backwards, trying to tip him off balance, exposing his chest to Lowe.

The human threw her and she cried out as she landed hard on her back.

Lowe joined her, bellowing as the male shot him at point-blank range in his side, just above his left hip. He swung with his right paw as pain blurred his vision and growled as he missed his target, landed hard intending to take another swing at the human, but his right front leg gave out beneath him and he sank against the dirt.

The male was quick to grab Cameo, twisting his left hand into her hair and dragging her up by it as he shoved the handgun into her face.

Lowe lay as still as he could manage on the ground, pretending to be out for the count so the man wouldn't put a bullet in his head, buying himself time to come up with a plan. He needed to save Cameo. The man wouldn't kill her—he knew that in his gut. He needed Cameo alive to face his boss, Karl.

She would be safe until then.

It was hard to get it through to both his bear side and the man in him though. Both sides wanted to rip the thug to shreds. Attacking him while he was holding Cameo would be too dangerous though. The man might end up shooting her.

He needed a better plan.

And the only one he could come up with was one that might cost him everything.

But if it meant saving her, it would be worth it.

CHAPTER 16

Cameo locked up tight as the man jammed the gun into her face, his hazel eyes as cold as ice.

"Tell me where the money is," he growled.

She swallowed hard and struggled to breathe, shut down the desire to tell the man to go to hell or admit she didn't have the money they wanted from her. She tried to think of a way out of this mess and couldn't stop her eyes from straying to the huge bear that lay on the ground just to her right.

Something deep inside her, something that made her feel as if she had lost her mind or had taken one too many pain pills, said that bear wasn't just a bear.

She stared at the wound on the animal's right shoulder.

The exact place where the man had shot Lowe with the rifle.

The only place the man had shot the bear was in its stomach. Maybe the man had caught the bear with a stray bullet when he had been firing upon her. That made the most sense to her, but that feeling screamed that he hadn't. It screamed that the bear was Lowe.

"I said, tell me where the fucking money is." The man shoved the barrel of the handgun into her jaw and she flinched, her eyes leaping away from the pool of blood forming beneath the bear to lock with his.

She stared at him, her thoughts racing and blurring, colliding until she couldn't think straight.

"Won't answer to me, then you'll answer to Karl. Got a message that he's in town and heading this way. Says he can't wait to see you again.

Reckon he can get you to talk." The man seized her by her nape and gripped it so hard her spine hurt. He pressed the gun into her temple and pushed her forwards. "Walk."

She shuffled her left foot forwards, desperately trying to come up with a plan as fear began to get the better of her again, swamping her mind with images of her bound and beaten, killed by her ex-boyfriend.

Cameo glanced at the rifle on the ground to her left, sickness sweeping through her as she considered lunging for it and using it on the man. He would probably shoot her before she could reach it, but she had to do something.

Before she could decide whether to make an attempt to get the rifle or not, the bear loosed a long, moaning noise and moved. That moan became a feral snarl as it lumbered onto its feet and turned towards her.

Cameo could only stare as it rose onto its hind legs.

And transformed into a man.

Into Lowe.

The man's gun dropped from the side of her head, his grip on her loosening, and she realised that the revelation that Lowe could turn into a bear hadn't shocked only her.

"What the fuck?" the man behind her breathed.

Cameo shook herself out of her stupor, unwilling to waste this chance she had been given. She would consider how insane this all was later.

She knocked the man's gun away from her and lunged to her left, hurling herself at the rifle. Shock rolled through her again as she managed to get her hands on it and twisted with it, onto her back, and aimed it at the man.

Who had his gun aimed right at Lowe.

"I don't know what the hell is going on here, but if you shoot me, I'll nail this freak between the eyes this time." The man turned a black look on her and slightly depressed the trigger of the gun he gripped.

Cameo swallowed hard and looked between him and Lowe. Her hands shook as she kept the gun aimed at the man, torn between surrendering and shooting him. She didn't want to give up, knew deep in her heart that if she released the gun that the man would go ahead and shoot Lowe anyway.

But if she didn't.

She looked at Lowe where he stood in the clearing, naked and bleeding badly from his right shoulder and a spot above his left hip.

"Shoot the bastard," he snarled. "I'll live."

She swallowed and raised the gun, aimed down the sights and hesitated. Her hands shook so violently that the end of the barrel jittered all over the place and her palms dampened, making it hard to keep hold of the gun. She didn't want Lowe to be shot again. He was clearly not like her, not human, and seemed confident that he could survive another bullet, but what if the man kept his word and shot him in the head?

She wasn't sure he could survive that.

She looked at him, guilt flaring inside her, an apology balanced on her lips. She couldn't do it. She couldn't risk him being killed.

She shrieked as something exploded from the bushes behind her, fumbled with the gun as Knox thundered past her, a blur of black, and held her breath as the man swung his gun towards Knox and squeezed the trigger.

Everything happened so fast.

The loud crack of a gun firing startled her.

The fierce recoil of the rifle had her falling on her back.

Knox rolled as another gunshot rang out, ending up in a crouch next to his brother.

Adrenaline surged through her as she gripped the rifle, still staring at the end of the barrel as it lightly smoked. Her hands shook harder, every inch of her trembling as her eyes slowly widened, as what she had done gradually dawned on her.

Someone grunted.

Someone growled like a beast.

Cameo tossed the rifle away from her and sat up, desperately looking for Lowe and Knox. Knox had the man pinned to the ground, his hand wrapped around his throat, but she didn't think it was necessary. The man wasn't going anywhere.

He struggled for each breath as blood pumped from the wound on his chest, forming sickening rivulets over his black jacket.

The man grinned, exposing bloodied teeth, and lowered his hazel eyes to lock with hers. "This... isn't over. You'll... get what's... coming... to you... *bitch*."

He sagged into the dirt.

Knox's head whipped towards her, his blue gaze darker than she had ever seen it. "What the hell does he mean by that?"

Lowe stepped up beside him, clutching his side, and looked from the dead man to her. "Karl is coming. He knows where we are."

"How?" Knox snarled.

Cameo swallowed hard. "My pack. I had a GPS in it. He might have returned to the road and called in the coordinates."

Knox cursed, shoved to his feet and looked at Lowe, something crossing his eyes that she didn't like. Lowe didn't like it either. He shook his head and went to seize hold of his brother's arm, but grimaced as he tried to do it with his right hand. He pressed his left hand to the wound on the right side of his chest and stared at Knox as his brother backed away from him.

"I'll head them off. I'll keep them away from the Creek and the Ridge." Knox kept backing away, even as Lowe limped towards him. "I'll lead them somewhere quiet and deal with them."

"No." Lowe gritted his teeth, his jaw flexing. His fair eyebrows furrowed and fear lit his sapphire eyes, making her feel awful, because she was responsible for everything that was happening.

She should have left the moment the weather had cleared, shouldn't have stuck around and got caught up in Lowe and the belief that he could help her. He had helped her, but at what cost?

His tone turned desperate as he reached for his brother with his bloodied left hand. "Just give me a minute. I'll get some clothes. We can go together."

Knox's expression hardened, but there was warmth in his blue eyes as he shook his head, a wealth of love that made Cameo feel even guiltier about what he was doing. "You need to heal... and you need to take care of her."

That only made her feel worse. The man had been here because of her. Karl was coming because of her. And now Knox was bravely heading out to face him alone.

Because of her.

He went to turn away and then pivoted to face Lowe again, closed the distance between them in two strides and wrapped his left hand around his brother's nape. He drew Lowe to him and pressed his forehead to his.

"Warn Saint and the others." Knox's eyes and his tone softened as he stared at Lowe. "And take care of yourself."

Lowe lifted his hand to cup Knox's nape too.

But he was already gone.

CHAPTER 17

Lowe stared in the direction his brother had gone, his chest feeling hollower by the second as he tracked Knox with his senses and the distance between them grew. The urge to follow him was strong and had him taking a step forwards, but he clenched his fists and stopped himself. Knox was right. He wasn't in any condition to fight and he needed to warn the others.

And take care of Cameo.

Her gaze drilled into his bare back, heating his skin, drawing his focus to her.

He waited, sure that she would say something, aware that she had seen him shift back from a bear and that she knew what he was now.

But she said nothing, just stood there staring at him, and worry for Knox began to transform into worry for her. He looked over his shoulder at her, and that worry only intensified as he saw how distant her gaze was and how pale she was.

She shook her head, causing the tangled threads of her brown-to-gold hair to brush her shoulders, and her eyes sharpened. They dropped to her body. She reached for the waist of her black sweatpants, pulling her cream sweater out of the way.

"You should take these. They're yours." She went to untie the laces of the sweatpants.

"No." He limped a step towards her, grimaced as his wounds hurt, and shook his head. "I can handle the cold."

Her brow furrowed and her eyes drifted down to his chest. They widened as she stared at it, horror crossing her delicate features, and she absently lifted her hand, flexed her fingers and then dropped it to her side and looked away from him.

"We need to get you somewhere warm," she murmured, sounding distant again, and refused to look at him.

Lowe swallowed the lump that formed in his throat as he looked at her, as he couldn't deny the part of him that whispered that it was over. He had ruined everything by shifting. Now Cameo would leave him. Could he really blame her?

Her gaze strayed to the dead man, the edge her eyes gained making him feel she was in shock.

As soon as it wore off, she was going to panic and run.

Could he use the time he had before that happened to convince her to stay with him and make her see that he would never hurt her, and that his being a bear shifter didn't mean they couldn't be together? It was worth a shot. He couldn't just let her go without a fight.

Her eyes gradually widened, the horror in them increasing as she continued to stare at the dead man.

"Cameo." He limped another step towards her, needing to be close to her and aching to take away the pain he could feel in her, hurt and guilt that trickled into him through their fragile bond.

"There's no getting around it this time," she whispered, her gaze losing focus, the panic he could sense in her mounting. "I killed a man. I need to turn myself in."

Lowe shook his head as fear blasted through him, the thought of Cameo leaving him swift to rouse a fierce need to keep her with him, to make her stay. He couldn't lose her.

"I can't let you do that." He risked another step towards her.

This time, her eyes darted to him. "I broke the law."

Lowe eased his left hand up, the need to touch her and take hold of her too strong to deny, even when he feared he might spook her into running. "The law... Cameo, if you go to the authorities... There are people who hunt my kind. They have eyes and ears everywhere. They'll come here. I can't let that happen. I can't let you turn yourself in. I can't let you go to prison… I just can't."

Disbelief filled her sky-blue eyes. "But I killed a man."

He risked it, seized hold of her arm and gripped it gently, hoping not to scare her. "In self-defence. But they won't care about that. They'll label you a murderer and rather than Karl and his fucking lackeys going to prison, you will. Cameo… I can't let that happen. Please?"

He brushed his thumb over her arm, shifting the soft cream material against her skin, and searched her eyes, staring deep into them, needing her to see how much the thought of her going to prison was killing him.

When he had told her to shoot the man, some part of him had known she wouldn't be able to do it. She was too kind. Too gentle. Too damn law-abiding. He had hoped that her threatening the man would have been enough to make him react, giving Lowe an opening. Instead, Knox had done that, and Cameo had reacted on instinct.

She had wanted to protect both him and his brother, and she had taken the shot.

He lifted his hand to her face and cupped her cheek, keeping her eyes on his. "I'm sorry I made you shoot that man."

Tears lined her dark lashes and her eyes strayed to her left, to the dead man, and then back to his. "I'm sorry too. I'm sorry I ever came here."

Pain lanced his heart and he dropped his hand from her face, the hurt quick to roll through him to fill every inch of him, to make every fibre of his being cry out.

The regret in her eyes cut him deeper than any blade could have, carved a hole in his heart and had him turning away from her. He busied himself with gathering the guns, not wanting her to see his pain, how the thought of her leaving and that she regretted meeting him was tearing him apart.

Lowe sucked down a breath, turned back to face her but couldn't bring himself to look her in the eye. "We should go."

She nodded and waited for him to reach her before she pivoted on her heel and hobbled along beside him. His hip ached with each step, but the cold air numbed his skin enough that he didn't feel the pain of his injuries. Or maybe it was the thought of Cameo leaving that numbed him to it.

He looked in the direction Knox had gone. Gods, he hoped his brother played it safe and didn't do anything reckless. While he appreciated what Knox had done for him and for the sake of his fated mate, he hated the thought of him alone out in the valley, tracking dangerous men who would be armed to the teeth.

Lowe looked down at the guns he gripped and clenched his jaw, fear chilling his blood as he thought about his brother facing armed men. He needed to find him and help him, and he would. As soon as he was on the mend, he was heading out to hunt for Knox. He couldn't let his brother handle this alone.

Besides, he had the feeling that he wasn't going to have a reason to stay at the Ridge soon.

He glanced at Cameo.

She was going to leave him.

The walk back to the clearing seemed to take forever, the air between him and Cameo growing heavier as she remained silent and he couldn't find his voice. There were a thousand things he wanted to tell her and he was sure they would go a long way towards convincing her to stay with him, but he couldn't get his thoughts straight as her words constantly echoed around his mind.

She was sorry she had come here.

"I understand." Those words slipped from him and it felt good to have them out there, to break the silence.

Cameo glanced at him. Stopped dead when her eyes landed on his face.

Her eyebrows rose. "Understand what?"

He looked across at her, gathered his courage and pushed the words out, forcing himself to face whatever fate awaited him, even when it was one he didn't want—a life without Cameo.

"You're sorry you came here and I understand... I get that—"

She stiffened and cut him off. "I don't think you do. I didn't mean it like that. Oh God, Lowe. I didn't mean it like that. I meant that I'm sorry I dragged you and everyone at Black Ridge into this mess and... got you hurt. And now Knox—"

"Knox will be fine." He put force behind those words, trying to make himself believe it, and stepped up to her. "As for me... Cameo, I'd go through trials a thousand times worse if it meant I got to meet you."

Her blue eyes softened, warmed in a way that warmed him too, but guilt lingered in their depths. He wasn't sure how to take that away for her. Or maybe he was. If she saw he was healing and if Knox returned unharmed, having dealt with her problem and put an end to things, he was sure that she would feel better.

Lowe lifted his hand and brushed his knuckles across her cheek, lost himself in the affection her eyes held and dared to hope that things might work out after all. He might not lose her. He might have his fated mate.

Forever with Cameo sounded like heaven to him.

He knew that was a long way off though, that convincing her to be his mate wasn't going to be easy. She was human and it would take time for her to accept what he was—if she could accept it—and a bond with him.

His senses warned that someone was approaching them.

Lowe turned and resisted the temptation to guide Cameo behind him, mostly because the male who came rushing to him wasn't alone. Holly hurried beside Saint, her cheeks rosy from the cold and her grey-green eyes bright as they landed on Cameo and then him.

The relief that filled them was quick to give way as she looked at him.

Saint growled, the vicious snarl pealing from his lips as he bared emerging fangs at Lowe, as if he was responsible for the fact his mate had just come running up to a naked male.

Holly was quick to toss a blanket in Lowe's face and turn to Saint. "I didn't see a thing."

Saint scowled down at her, his eyes dark and filled with a look that said he didn't believe that for a second. He huffed and slid Lowe a black look.

Lowe wrapped the blanket around his chest and tucked the end in, wearing it like a dress. Damn, it felt good to be covered, and not only because it stopped Saint from looking as if he wanted to rip him apart. The warmth of the blanket felt luxurious and he wanted to stand there and savour it for a moment, but a glance at Cameo had worry rushing through him again.

Cameo eased a step forwards, staring at Saint as if she was in a trance. Her voice was distant as she murmured, "I thought maybe the stress or the pain medication... you..."

She looked over her shoulder at Lowe.

"I'm not going crazy. You were a bear... right?"

He swallowed hard and reached for her, the panic flooding him quick to flow away as she didn't try to evade him or run. She let him take hold of her arm, let him step up to her, closing the gap between them.

"I have a little explaining to do." He stroked her arm, lifted his hand to her face and palmed her cheek. "We'll get you warmed up and settled down again, and then I'll tell you everything."

And he meant everything.

Part of him had thought he would never have the mate talk, but it loomed on the horizon, and gods, he was dreading it. Saint was lucky that his fated female had turned out to be another shifter, someone already familiar with their world.

"Where's Knox?" Saint looked beyond Lowe and then back at him.

Lowe's stomach dropped and his heart ached as he reached out with his senses and couldn't feel his brother with them. He rubbed at his sternum as that ache worsened when he thought about what his brother was doing.

"We managed to take the man down." He neglected to mention it was Cameo who had shot him because he felt sure she wouldn't like to be reminded of what she had done. He didn't want her talking about going to the authorities again. "The man revealed more were coming. Knox went to head them off."

Saint nodded in the direction of the Ridge. "Come on. We'll talk more about it when we have you both warmed up."

Lowe wrapped his good arm around Cameo and helped her, limping with her back to the clearing. He had never been so happy or so scared to see his cabin as it came into view. His heart thundered, the thought of having to sit Cameo down and tell her everything making him shake a little.

She glanced up at him. "Are you cold?"

He shook his head and met her gaze. He wasn't sure what to say to her. If he admitted he was nervous, would it make her soften towards him? Maybe make it easier for him to convince her that his being a bear shifter wasn't a bad thing? Admitting he was nervous felt a little like he was confessing he was guilty about something though. At least, he was sure that was what she would make of it.

The two big males striding towards them provided a good distraction, had Cameo tensing and tucking closer to him when she noticed them.

"It's okay," he murmured and rubbed her arm. "It's just Rune and Maverick."

And damn, it felt good to see the two of them.

Maverick cut an imposing figure dressed in a black wool coat that reached his knees, hugging his athletic frame, and equally dark jeans. His onyx hair was wild on top, as if he had been running his hand through it, and his clear grey eyes held a sharp edge as he stormed towards them.

But Lowe figured it was Rune who had made Cameo lock up tight.

The big six-seven male looked every bit the fighter he was with his dark hair cut close to his scalp, the scar that darted up from his left temple into his hair clearly visible, and a black woollen sweater moulded to his broad chest and huge biceps like a second skin. He clenched his fists, causing his forearms to flex, and his expression darkened, his ice-blue eyes growing as frigid as a glacier when they narrowed on Cameo.

Lowe bared fangs at the male, warning him to take his eyes off her. While he was no match for Rune in a fight, it wouldn't stop him from attacking the male. Cameo was his. He tugged her a little closer, that action enough to have Rune shifting his cold gaze to Saint.

"What's up?" Saint looked from Rune to Maverick, asking what was on Lowe's mind too.

The two bears often looked as if they were on edge, but this felt different to him, and he had the feeling it wasn't because there was a human female—Cameo—at the Ridge.

"We're not the only arrivals." Maverick's deep voice was a low growl as he shoved his fingers through his hair. "Scented four males and a female at the trailhead."

Cameo whispered, "Karl."

Maverick slid her a dark look. "Who's Karl? Someone to do with you? Figure you're the one who got my pride into this mess."

Rather than shrinking back against Lowe, she stood her ground, but Lowe could feel the fear in her, together with the guilt.

"Back down, Maverick," Saint growled before Lowe could say anything and the big black-haired bear immediately backed off, his gaze shifting to him.

"Knox has gone to head them off and lead them away from the Ridge and the Creek." Lowe's chest constricted as he thought about his brother out there, unaware of what he was up against.

Four males and a female. All of them were probably armed too.

Knox was going to have to be damned careful about dealing with them if he was going to survive this, and Lowe had the terrible fear that his twin wouldn't take the necessary precautions, would try to deal with them quickly and all at once.

"Knox will be fine." Saint came to him and clutched his left shoulder, lightly squeezing it.

Lowe looked at him, catching the belief he heard in those words in his eyes, and then at the others. Rune and Maverick looked as if they believed the same thing. He glanced at Cameo.

Guilt shone in her blue eyes and she lowered them to her feet, avoiding his gaze.

Lowe turned to her as Saint stepped back. He gently touched her chin, pressing two fingers to it and lifting it up. She still wouldn't look at him.

"This isn't your fault, Cameo." He wanted to make the others leave, but knew in his heart that they wouldn't. His pride stuck together and none of them would want to leave him out here alone with only a human female for company when he was injured, exposed and vulnerable to attack.

She swallowed hard and glanced at him, her eyes leaping to lock with his before they darted away again. "It is. I got you all involved in my problem and now Knox is out there—"

"Knox can handle these people." And this time he believed that. His brother was strong, brave, and a fighter. He was clever too. As much as he feared that Knox would go in there with metaphorical guns blazing, he knew deep in his soul that he wouldn't.

Knox would scout the group and come up with a plan, would find a way to divide and conquer the enemy.

"He'll be back before any of us knows it and he'll probably have some wild tales to tell us, all of which will sound a little too tall to believe… but they'll probably be one hundred percent true." He feathered his fingers along her jaw as she finally looked at him, her eyes colliding with his, and hope shone in hers. Hope he felt deep in his heart. "Come on. Let's get warmed up."

She lifted her hand and brushed her fingers over his chest, close to the bullet wound. "We should take care of this."

Maverick opened his mouth to say something and Lowe shot him down with a glare, fearing that the male was about to offer his services in that department. He wanted to be alone with Cameo, could feel she needed a moment to breathe, without his friends surrounding her. She needed to be alone with him. He needed that too.

Because Knox wasn't the only one facing a tough battle, one that might end badly for him.

Lowe gathered his courage, aware he was going to need it.

Stared into Cameo's eyes.

"We need to talk."

CHAPTER 18

"We need to talk."

Cameo had never heard more ominous words. They rattled around her head as she helped Lowe back to his cabin, as the other men and Holly left them alone at the steps to the deck. Saint gave Lowe a look she could easily interpret, one that said Lowe wasn't the only one who wanted to talk about something.

She limped up the steps to the deck, managed a smile as Lowe opened the door for her. She hobbled inside and straight over to her pain meds, picked them up and stared at them. The logical part of her brain had convinced her that the pills were responsible for the fact she had seen Lowe transform from a bear into a man, and it still clung to that. The thought that he might actually be able to change forms was far too out there for her tired mind to grasp, but she tried to make it sink in.

Tried to make herself believe it.

Partly because she was hoping this talk Lowe wanted to have revolved around that fact.

It struck her that she had been right to feel Black Ridge had a secret, and it was one that she never would have guessed.

One that blew her mind.

Everyone here could turn into a bear at will.

He sank onto the couch, a weary sigh escaping his lips, and she closed the door and looked at him. He was pale. A little too pale. She glanced at the blood that covered his chest on the right side and had soaked into the beige blanket near his hip too, and sickness swelled inside her. She swallowed the bile that rose into her throat and steeled her nerves, focused on taking care of him and pushed everything else to the back of her mind. Right now, tending to his wounds took priority.

Maybe she was just trying to pretend her world hadn't taken a sharp turn towards crazy out in the woods.

"Do you think… I think we should call Yasmin." She looked over her shoulder at the door and considered going out to find Saint to ask him to get the doctor for Lowe.

She looked back at him.

Lowe shook his head and sat up a little, his lips pulling taut as pain flared in his eyes. If he had been trying to make himself look less like he was knocking on Death's door by sitting up, it hadn't gone to plan. He grimaced and dabbed at his shoulder with his fingers.

Sighed.

"It'll heal." He swallowed hard and his hand dropped to his lap.

It would, but it was going to take days and if a bullet was still inside him, he might get sick. Could he get sick? She looked at the pill bottle in her hand, tempted to offer him one.

Lowe glanced at her, a look in his eyes that made her want to go to him, because he looked as if he expected her to run from him.

She wasn't going anywhere.

As crazy as this place was, she wanted to be here.

With him.

And it wasn't because Karl was out there looking for her.

Being here with Lowe felt right. As if she belonged by his side. She might feel as if she was going mad, had imagined half of what she had seen, but she was sure of one thing.

She had fallen for Lowe.

And she had fallen hard.

When she boiled it down, the fact that Lowe was different to her didn't change a thing. She gazed at him, seeing the same man she had met in the forest that night—a noble, kind, and wonderful man.

"Do you have a med kit?" She wanted to smile when her words seemed to startle him, had his eyes widening and a look of disbelief flitting across his handsome face. "I said I wanted to take care of your injuries. Remember? If you won't let me ask Saint to go for the doctor, then I'll have to do."

"I do... just..." His throat worked on another hard swallow and he gestured towards a cupboard. "Black bag."

He hadn't believed her. He had thought that as soon as they were alone that she would run from him, as if he was some big bad monster she should fear. There wasn't a monster before her. There was only Lowe. Only the man she loved.

A man who needed her help.

A man who had bravely fought to protect her.

A man who had kept his promise to her. He had kept her safe. He had taken care of her. And now she could see in his eyes that he wanted to take care of the rest of her problem and deal with Karl. She couldn't let that happen. Even once his wounds were bound, Lowe would be in no fit state to go out into the cold and up against five people. Knox was right about that.

For his twin's sake and hers, she would keep him in this cabin, even when part of her wanted to be out there too, facing her problem and dealing with it.

Cameo found the bag and went to Lowe, settled the med kit on the couch beside him and focused on her task. She checked the wound on his shoulder first, grimacing as she moved around behind him and found an exit hole that was ragged and had tracked blood down his back. An exit wound was a good thing though.

She tried to recall her training and as it all came back to her, she sank into it, moving methodically from one step to the next. Using taking care of him to clear her mind and give this strange turn of events time to sink in. First, she cleaned the wounds. Then, she checked them, inspecting them more closely. Satisfied she couldn't see any shrapnel from the bullet and the fact the bleeding had already slowed to a crawl, she cleaned around the wound again and covered it with a large dressing. She carefully smoothed the sticky edges down against his chest, her gaze tracking her fingers as guilt flared again.

Lowe lifted his left hand and caught her wrist. She glanced at him, got snagged in the soft look he was giving her.

"Don't blame yourself." He shook his head slightly.

How was that even possible? Lowe had been badly hurt because of her and if he had been human, like her, he probably would have died from this wound. Her gaze dropped to his hip. He certainly would have died from that one.

"You didn't hurt me, Cameo. The man did."

She sank to her backside on the couch beside him. A man she had killed. Lowe was right. It had been in part done in self-defence and in part done to protect another person and stop them from being killed, but she had still killed a man. Two men.

"What you did... it doesn't make you a bad person. It doesn't change who you are." Lowe stroked his thumb over the inside of her wrist, belief ringing in his deep voice, luring her gaze back to his. His blond eyebrows furrowed as he stared into her eyes. "Cameo..."

Pain surfaced in his eyes. Fear there too. His hand shook against hers again and she swore she could feel he was nervous. Maybe she was the nervous one.

Because she was about to take a leap.

"What you are, Lowe..." She clutched his wrist as he tried to draw his hand away from her, the fear winning in his eyes. She stopped him from distancing himself. She wasn't out to hurt him. She only wanted to make him feel better. "That's who you are and it doesn't... it doesn't change how I feel about you."

"It doesn't?" His blue eyes softened, a hopeful edge to them. "You... Cameo, I know this is all a lot to take in and it's what I wanted to talk to you about. This place... everyone here—"

"Can turn into a bear." She put it out there for him, hating the sight of him struggling and the fear that began to fill his eyes again. "Were you bitten by one and this just happened or... were you born like this."

"I was born like this. We all were." He tried to shift to face her and grimaced, his other hand falling to his side.

Cameo cursed herself for forgetting about his other wound. She gathered the necessary supplies, set them on the couch between them, and undid the blanket he had tucked around himself. It pooled in his lap, revealing his chest down to his hips, and she glanced at him.

Caught the fact the nerves that had been in his eyes were gone now. Because she was occupying herself with his injuries again and wasn't talking about the fact he was a bear-man or because she wasn't running?

She figured it was a bit of both, but she couldn't stay silent. She could however make this easier on him by busying herself rather than staring at him while she talked about what he was.

"So this place is like your sanctuary? You're all bear-men in a kind of... pack?" She grimaced at her poor choice of words as she cleaned the wound above his hip.

"Bear shifters, and it's a pride. Wolves have packs. The rest of us have prides." He tensed and a glance at him revealed it wasn't because she had hurt him. The awkward and worried look on his face said it was because he had just revealed bears weren't the only shifters in this world.

"Wolves. Like werewolves?" She stared into his eyes, finding that oddly easy to believe, surprised by how it made all of it much easier to believe when she thought about Lowe and the others as werebears.

Only she didn't think they changed during a full moon and howled at it.

He nodded. "Wolf shifters are a little divided on that though. Some like to be called werewolves and others prefer to be called wolf shifters. Me and my kin just call them wolves."

She frowned and pursed her lips as she thought about what other shifters might be out there. Her eyebrows rose.

"Is Holly a bear or a wolf?"

"She's a cougar."

Cameo's eyebrows shot up as something hit her. "That's what you meant when you said you wanted to kill the cougars. Your neighbours are cougar... shifters."

She hoped she had that right. Werecougars just sounded weird. She wanted to chuckle at that. If the thing she found weird was the name they gave their species, then she really had lost her mind. Or everything was sinking in and beginning to make sense to her.

Something else dawned on her.

"Oh my God. The bear. The bear that was bleeding everywhere." She stared at Lowe, stunned as she thought about it. "That was Saint."

Lowe nodded, but his features pinched in a way that made her feel he was worried about things again. He was tense for a few seconds, until she looked back down at what she was doing and started cleaning his wound again.

He loosed a long sigh as he relaxed. "You need to know what you're getting into if you're going to stay."

"I'm going to stay." She put that out there before her nerve failed her and glanced up at his face.

"I know. For now." He went to look away from her.

"Not for now." She rushed that confession out before he could say anything and his gaze locked with hers, his eyes widening.

"Not for now?"

She shook her head.

"I will understand if you want to leave. I won't try to make you stay." He had that defeated look again.

Cameo didn't like it. It wasn't like him. The man she knew was gentle, but a warrior too.

"You're not going to fight for me?" She canted her head, her fingers pausing at her work, pressing softly to his damp skin just above his waist. "If I walked out that door right now, you'd just let me go?"

A flicker of something in his eyes told her that he didn't want that. He didn't want her to leave him. She didn't want him to let her go.

She felt bad provoking him, pushing him, but she wanted to know how he felt about her. She wanted to know that he wanted her here, needed her with him as badly as she needed to be with him.

A war erupted in his blue eyes and she watched it unfold, could almost hear his thoughts as he went back and forth about what he would do.

An ache started in her heart, born of a whisper that drifted through her mind, too quiet for her to hear but it stirred a feeling in her, and she was sure that once it grew loud enough it would devastate her.

Lowe vanquished it before it could fully form.

He clutched her hand and stared deep into her eyes. "I'd fight. I can't let you go. I meant that. Gods, I mean it. I would do whatever it took to keep you by my side because I'm crazy about you... I know this is fast... but... I love you, Cameo, and that means that if you wanted to leave—"

She silenced him with a soft kiss, unable to bear seeing him in pain, seeing him torn between doing anything to keep her with him because he loved her and doing nothing to hurt her.

Because he loved her.

Her noble bear.

The thought that he would let her leave because he loved her, that he would break his own heart, made hers ache for him. Made her love him all the more. If that was possible. She wasn't sure it was.

He clutched her nape and kissed her, keeping it gentle and tender, filled with love that warmed her to her soul.

Lowe pulled back before she was ready, and she worried it was because his injuries were hurting him when she looked into his eyes and saw the pain that shone in them.

"Are they hurting?" She lowered her hand to his hip, checked it over and then tried to see the other side of the wound. "Are you sure you don't need me to get Yasmin?"

He shook his head, his blond eyebrows slowly furrowing as he stared at her face.

She gently pressed her hand to his side and he shuffled forwards a few inches, so she could see the exit wound. She carefully cleaned and inspected it, covered it with a dressing and then eased him back again. She looked at the bullet hole in his stomach and swallowed hard. What if either of the bullets had hit something vital? She could dress them, but if the one that had penetrated his side had nicked an organ or his intestines, he might get sick. Terribly sick.

Just the thought of that happening was enough to have her worried, feeling frantic with a need to make sure it wasn't the case.

She looked at him. "You said you could call an air ambulance."

He shook his head and frowned at her. "No hospitals. I'll be fine, Cameo, shifters don't get sick like humans... but if it will set your mind at ease, I'll get Yasmin to look at the wounds."

"Is she a cougar shifter too?"

Another shake. "She's a goddess."

Cameo stared at him, her mind blanking as she tried to process that. There weren't just shifter breeds in this world with the humans. There were goddesses too. Which meant there were gods. And what else was living undetected among humans?

Not quite undetected.

"You mentioned hunters." She frowned into his eyes. "Are they the reason you won't go to a hospital?"

He nodded and swallowed hard. "I can't risk exposing my pride to them. We have to be careful about everything we do. There's an organisation out there that does terrible things to people like us. Experiments. Torture. Raids that often end with most of a pride dead."

"That's awful." She wouldn't mention hospitals again or anything to do with humans. She stilled. "Lowe... I'm human. The way that man looked at me... He doesn't want me here. He thinks I'm a threat or a liability."

"Maverick can go fuck himself," Lowe snarled and reached for her, slid his hand around her nape and gripped it gently as his eyes darted between hers, softening again. "You're staying. He understands that. He knows the reason I need you here."

"Because you love me?" She wanted to hear him admit that again.

He sighed. "Because I love you, and—"

"And?" She shuffled a little closer to him when he looked as if he didn't want to continue. She was damned if he was going to leave her hanging, leave her wondering what he had been going to say, especially when he looked so torn. So afraid. She raised her hands and gently framed his face. "Tell me, Lowe. Whatever it is, it can't make this whole thing any crazier."

He looked as if he doubted that.

Dropped his gaze to his knees and heaved another sigh, and she frowned as she felt sure he was nervous. He wasn't shaking and he wasn't looking at her. Nothing about him betrayed his nerves. How was it she could feel these things about him? It was like a sixth sense.

"There's a reason…" He sucked down another breath and exhaled hard as his eyes darted up to lock with hers. "There's a reason I felt compelled to find you the night you were attacked in the woods. When I scented your blood… I didn't realise it at the time, but as I fell for you, as we grew closer, it hit me. We're fated."

"Fated?" She lost herself in the calm blue of his eyes.

A warm blue.

There was so much affection in his gaze as he looked at her, mixed with a dash of hope and a hefty dose of fear. Because he was afraid that what he needed to tell her would scare her off?

It wasn't going to happen.

He nodded. "Shifters… We have fated mates. A true mate. Someone we feel was made for us and we can share a powerful bond with them."

A bond.

Something suddenly made sense.

Over the days she had spent with Lowe, she had begun to feel as if what they shared was special, a once in a lifetime kind of love and a deep and powerful connection. Things between them had felt intense, as if someone had turned the volume up to eleven on everything he made her feel.

Because she was his fated mate.

"You look… shocked." He grimaced. "I'm rushing this and not doing a good job."

She shook her head. "I'm not shocked. In fact, a lot of things just clicked into place and made sense. From the moment we met, I felt drawn to you. Something about you made me… wild… a little reckless. I felt— This is going to sound crazy. I feel incredibly protective of you and, well, I can't seem to get enough of you."

A stunned look crossed his face.

"You feel it too? I mean, I wasn't sure you would. You're human… Not like I know much about how a human should feel in this situation, but I figured... Well, it doesn't really matter what I figured now, does it?" A small smile tugged at the corners of his lips. "You think this potential bond makes you reckless and wild, you should see it from my side. I'm insanely possessive of you, want to lash out at any male who so much as looks at you, and I really can't get enough of you. Hell, right now, I just want to gather you into my arms and spend the rest of the day kissing you."

She smiled at him. He was rambling, but it was good to see him relaxing. It made her relax too, made everything feel normal again, back to how it had been before she had discovered that he was a bear shifter. She still had so many questions to ask him about that, was sure she was going to spend the next few weeks, if not months, suddenly thinking of something else she wanted to know about his kind.

But right now, she wanted to know one thing.

"You keep mentioning a bond. What does that mean?"

His face lost all warmth, his skin paling as his smile faltered. He ran a hand over his hair, mussing the golden threads of it, and grimaced.

"Cameo... we're fated and that means..." He huffed, sank back against the couch and then sat up again, agitated now.

She placed her hand on his knee, wanting to show him that he could tell her. It wasn't going to change how she felt about him. She wasn't going to run.

His eyes locked with hers. "I'm driven to mate with you."

"Like sex?" She shrugged at that thought, because she wasn't going to turn down sex with Lowe. It was hardly a chore. In fact, there was a part of her—a wicked part—that wanted him right now. The sensible part overruled it, pointing out that he was injured. Wicked part just pointed out that she could be on top.

"More than sex. When we..." A blush climbed his cheeks. "I have a powerful urge to bite your nape, and if I do, it'll trigger a need in you to do the same. But you don't have to bite me." He rushed those words out, his eyes widening as he shook his head. "Only I have to bite you and that... that will bind us as mates."

Oh.

Her eyebrows rose as she let that sink in, and he wasn't the only one blushing when she remembered how she had clawed at his nape when they had made love, unable to deny the wicked need to mark him there. At the time, she had put it down to a heat of the moment thing. Now, she had the feeling she had wanted to mark him. She had wanted to trigger this bond she hadn't even known about.

Just thinking about him sinking his teeth into her nape had heat curling through her, something that surprised her. The thought of someone biting her should scare her, even disturb her, but it didn't. She felt hazy from head to toe, felt an overwhelming need to kiss him and seduce him.

Cameo tamped it down.

The heat that shone in Lowe's eyes said he had noticed her reaction though, and when he looked at her like that, she found it hard to resist the wicked needs rolling through her.

She cleared her throat and focused on what he had said, because she had seen a few horror movies in her time, and her sensible side was screaming a question at her.

"If you bite me... will you make me a bear too?"

He was quick to shake his head. "No. I can't. We're born like this, not made. Biting you won't turn you into a shifter, but it *will* change you. Your life will be tied to mine. You'll be stronger. You won't age. Won't get sick. Your senses will be sharper. You'll probably be faster too, and you'll heal quickly. You'll live as long as I do. We could have centuries together."

"That's quite the list of perks," she muttered and smiled as she couldn't hold back the words, needed to lighten the atmosphere a little because it was all beginning to feel terribly real. "Here I was thinking that amazing body and incredible smile were all you had to offer."

The right corner of his mouth quirked at that, causing a dimple in his cheek.

"You said that with a smile, so I'll let you off." He sobered, his eyes gaining a serious edge again. "This is a big decision. I know that. Even though it kills me because I want you to be my mate right this second...

You have all the time in the world to make your decision. If you want to be my mate one day, you only have to say the word."

She appreciated that he wasn't going to rush her, because he was right. It was a lot to take in and she needed to take things slowly, wanted this thing she had with Lowe to deepen and grow stronger before she took the next step, and wanted him to answer around three million questions. Even though her instincts were pushing her to mate with him, she was determined to take her time and learn all there was to know about his kind and his world, and once she had all the facts and felt she was ready, she would take the leap.

Cameo nodded and leaned towards him, kissed him softly and slowly, savouring the way he sighed as her lips danced across his, as if he was in heaven. She knew she was.

She drew back and stroked his bare chest as she looked deep into his eyes. "One day."

He smiled and she knew he had seen the promise in her eyes, one that came from her heart. She wouldn't keep him waiting long. She wasn't sure she could.

The sensible side of her lined up the first one hundred questions for him.

The wicked part of her shut it down.

She would start filling a mental binder with all the answers she needed tomorrow.

She leaned into him and kissed him again, gasped into his mouth as he slid his left arm around her waist and tugged her against him, pressing her chest to his. There was so much love in his kiss that she warmed down to her marrow, her heart growing lighter as she lost herself in it and in him, and in thoughts of the future she knew deep in her soul she wanted with him.

As his mate.

One day, she would bravely step into a wild new world to be with the man she loved with all her heart. It might be years. He kissed her deeper, igniting heat in her veins that burned that thought away. It might be months. She moaned and shivered as he drew her closer, his arm flexing against her back. Maybe weeks. Weeks at a minimum.

It might be weeks, but one day she would take the leap and become his mate. For him. For her. For them.

Forever.

One day.

Soon.

Possibly tomorrow.

The End

ABOUT THE AUTHOR

Felicity Heaton is a New York Times and USA Today best-selling author who writes passionate paranormal romance books. In her books she creates detailed worlds, twisting plots, mind-blowing action, intense emotion and heart-stopping romances with leading men that vary from dark deadly vampires to sexy shape-shifters and wicked werewolves, to sinful angels and hot demons!

If you're a fan of paranormal romance authors Lara Adrian, J R Ward, Sherrilyn Kenyon, Kresley Cole, Gena Showalter, Larissa Ione and Christine Feehan then you will enjoy her books too.

If you love your angels a little dark and wicked, her best-selling Her Angel romance series is for you. If you like strong, powerful, and dark vampires then try the Vampires Realm romance series or any of her stand alone vampire romance books. If you're looking for vampire romances that are sinful, passionate and erotic then try her London Vampires romance series. Or if you like hot-blooded alpha heroes who will let nothing stand in the way of them claiming their destined woman then try her Eternal Mates series. It's packed with sexy heroes in a world populated by elves, vampires, fae, demons, shifters, and more. If sexy Greek gods with incredible powers battling to save our world and their home in the Underworld are more your thing, then be sure to step into the world of Guardians of Hades.

If you have enjoyed this story, please take a moment to contact the author at **author@felicityheaton.com** or to post a review of the book online

Connect with Felicity:
Website – http://www.felicityheaton.com
Blog – http://www.felicityheaton.com/blog/
Twitter – http://twitter.com/felicityheaton
Facebook – http://www.facebook.com/felicityheaton
Goodreads – http://www.goodreads.com/felicityheaton
Mailing List – http://www.felicityheaton.com/newsletter.php

FIND OUT MORE ABOUT HER BOOKS AT:
http://www.felicityheaton.com